THE *Dirty Heroes* COLLECTION

NEVER
LOST

TL MAYHEW

The Black Fox, by Brianna Hale

Finding His Strength, by Measha Stone

While She Sleeps, by Dani René

Bound by Sacrifice, by Murphy Wallace

Never Lost, by TL Mayhew

The Curse Behind The Mask, by Holly J. Gill

Clockwork Stalker, by Cari Silverwood

Kiss and Tell, by Jo-Anne Joseph

Skeleton King, by Charity B.

Make Me Real, by Petra J. Knox

Cruel Water, by Dee Palmer

The Masked Prince, by Faith Ryan

Hunted, by Cassandra Faye

The Lady, by Golden Angel

Once upon a time, a scorned Queen opened
a box, unleashing horrible evil on the world's
heroes.

Instead of gallantry and chivalry, they now
possessed much more perverse traits. They've
fallen victim to their darkest and most deviant
desires.

This is one of their stories...

BLURB
Never Lost

Shadows are formed by objects blocking rays of light.

Just not mine.

Its darkness is ever-present, taunting me, tricking me into doing things a man should never do, but I've learned to embrace it.

Will she?

Lost in dreams of a life anywhere but here, she's ignorant to the danger perched just outside the window.

Taking her will be easy.

But can I teach her to fly?

Prologue

HIS FACE IS PLASTERED OVER EVERY TABLOID in the checkout line. A mix of both; professionally posed images, on the more reputable magazines, and shots taken from a considerable distance on the lesser-known rags. Each with its own version of what is going on in the life of yet another A-list celebrity.

Now the Most Eligible Bachelor in Hollywood.

Emotional Breakup for Our Beloved Preston.

Tinka Caught Kissing *A Life Lost in Neverland* **Producer.**

Preston and Tinka were once America's favorite on and off-screen couple. Cast in more than ten movies together they raked in millions, but as with many famous pairings, it ended almost as quickly as it started. The details of what happened between them is still somewhat of a mystery. Unreliable sources say infidelity played a part, while others say it was a mutual separation.

Whatever the reason, it hasn't hurt Preston's career. He's booked for three movies over the next five years and two new TV series that, if the pilots do well, will put him in long-term contracts.

Tinka, on the other hand, hasn't had it as easy. Against her agent's wishes, she began dating publicly before the breakup was officially announced. It put her in a negative light with everyone in the industry, except one—the paparazzi. They've had a field day snapping her picture every chance they get and in the most unflattering ways. With only one movie contract in the past year, her lavish style of living is at risk.

It's a sad tale of what could have been.

Faithful fans were devastated, posting crying GIFs and offering their sympathies on social media, all the while never giving up hope of a reconciliation. But not everyone felt the same. Some rallied around the idea of a breakup, because if Preston is single, there's the smallest chance they could have a turn with "The King of the Big Screen."

I can't blame them, with his dark hair, dark eyes, and a body chiseled from the side of a mountain; Preston Pace is a decadent god.

CHAPTER ONE
Winsley

*T*HE FRENCH MAID COSTUME GLIDES EASILY against my bare skin, puckering my nipples as he lifts it over my head.

Role-playing was his idea. Being an actor, he's the perfect teacher and he's more than happy to coach me along, but not because of what he does for a living, instead it's because tonight, I'll call him Sir.

Once the costume is in a puddle on the floor, he raises his hands and cups my face. Nothing could have prepared me for this moment.

His lips inches from mine.

His warm breath caressing my skin.

When our lips finally connect, the kiss weakens my knees both figuratively and literally, and now I'm looking up from my place at his feet.

Larger than life, he towers over me with crossed arms and a stare only the devil could have created. Our eyes lock, he gives me an approving nod, and I make quick work of loosening his belt and unfastening his pants. They drop to the floor with a light thud.

What lies beneath is long, thick, and intimidating but not beyond my abilities. "No pain, no gain. Isn't that what they say?" I mutter before relaxing my jaw, opening my mouth as wide as it will go and...

"He's hot, isn't he?" Jennifer asks, ripping the daydream from my mind like duct tape from skin.

The magazine falls to the floor and my face tints red. I shrug in response. "Eh, he's okay."

"Liar! You're totally into him, look at your face..." When she realizes just how much, her eyes go wide and her lips form a giant O, "... Wait, look at your face. What in God's name were you thinking about?"

"Nothing," I mutter, secretly eyeing the sexy smile shining back up at me from the floor.

"You're so full of shit. Tell me."

Picking the magazine up and tossing it back on the rack, I push the shopping cart forward and begin placing items on the rubber belt, ignoring her pressing look. If I don't, the daydream will surely gush out on a waterfall of words.

I've known Jennifer since we were in elementary school.

We both ended up in Los Angeles for different reasons, hers was an agent. Discovered at the tender age of nine, her acting career began early. Starring in commercials and kid shows, she was an instant hit. Mine, was my mother.

Seeing Jennifer's success, my mother was insistent on me following in my best friend's footsteps. Which meant picking up and moving across the country. Unfortunately for her, it never interested me as much as it did my best friend.

Until now.

"Okay, I guess I won't tell you about the open casting calls for extras on his next film, *A Taste of Yesteryear*," she retorts.

One sentence and I'm frozen in place. Did she say what I think she did? She couldn't have because it's not possible my luck could be this good. Being on the set of his movie could mean a chance at meeting the infamous Preston Pace, in actual fucking person.

"You're joking…right?" I ask, turning to face her. "Because if you are, I will strangle the life out of you right here in this store." My fingers circle around her neck, but she brushes me off with little effort.

Pointing a finger in my face, she confirms, "So you do like him. I knew it."

"Jennifer…" I warn.

Her grin goes wider. "I'm not joking but I'm also not telling you any details until you tell me what you were fantasizing about with Mr. Six-Pack Abs here," she says, slapping a cover with the back of her hand.

"Seriously? You're incorrigible."

"Seriously," she replies, crossing her arms.

It's a sign I'm not getting any further until I spill my thoughts. I could lie, give her some fluffy tale about picket fences and a family with two point three kids, but when you've been friends for as long as we have, she'd know I'm not being honest, so I tell her the truth. "I was thinking about him ripping off my French maid costume from Halloween last year. If you must know."

"Girl…I knew you were dirty, but damn.

You've been reading too many romance novels."

Or watching too many Preston movies, I think to myself.

"Maybe I shouldn't say anything, you might end up…"

"Will you just fucking tell me?" I whisper-shout.

"Ma'am?" A male voice sounds in the back of my mind.

"Okay, don't get your panties in a wad." She glances to the right and then back at me. "The casting site said Thursday at 6:00 a.m. I'm planning on trying out for one of the costars."

"That's in two days! When were you going to tell me?" I ask her, with a hand on my hip.

"Ma'am?" The voice again.

On a huff I look around Jennifer, where a heavy-set man leans against the handle of his cart. "You're holding up the line," he says flatly.

Jennifer laughs and nods behind me.

When I turn, I'm met with a bored stare from the cashier. What if they heard my confession? My cheeks tint red for the second time this morning. I don't know what is wrong with me; I haven't blushed this much in a single day—

ever. After apologizing profusely, first, to the man behind us and then to the cashier I move forward.

She's indifferent about my very existence, picking at her nails while she reads off the total. "Forty-six seventy-three."

Once I've paid, and placed all our things in the cart, we head for the door. "So, like were you going to just keep this to yourself?"

"I was waiting for the right time. When I saw you eye fucking the magazine, that's when I knew…it was the right time," she chuckles.

"Very funny, but seriously though?" I encourage, placing the items in the car.

She doesn't readily respond, instead she grabs the empty cart and pushes it into a bay. I suspect tempting me with the suspense of what exciting things she has to say.

Once we're both back in the car I twist in the seat and demand all the details. "Tell me everything."

The time of secrecy is over, and she's more than happy to fill me in, clapping her hands excitedly. "Yes! Okay, so my agent told me there were these casting calls online. She said I should visit the site, check out the story lines and if I liked any, I could put my name in. That's when I saw it, the post for extras. They're only looking for a limited number, like ten or something, and it's a restaurant scene, so you'd be inside. Not out in the elements. And you might be fake eating with some handsome actor, but that doesn't matter because you'll get to meet Mr. Preston Pace." She takes a breath then starts again, "You just have to do this Winsley, please."

"I don't know, Jen. I love you, and the thought of meeting him raises chill bumps all over my body, but it's been so long since I've done any acting," I explain, but the words coming out don't match what I'm feeling. My answer should be an immediate yes. Any chance at meeting Preston is one I shouldn't hesitate in taking, but I'm not sure I'm ready to live outside of my fantasy quite yet.

In my world he ticks all the boxes of the perfect man: respectful, funny, smart, and sexy. But what if we meet and he's a total asshole? I know it's not how they portray him in the media. It's a given they'll say whatever they're told and then some. All it takes is a good PR rep and a few nice words. I'm just not ready my dreams to be shattered yet.

"You eat, don't you?"

"Yeah…" I answer with creased brows, wondering where she's going with this.

"And you know how to converse with others, right?" she asks, somehow with a straight face.

I roll my eyes.

"That, my lovely, lovely friend, is all the acting you'll need to do." She takes my hand in hers and flutters long lashes over big brown eyes. "Please."

On a deep sigh, I drop my head back to the seat. "Don't make me regret this."

Without warning, she leans over and kisses me on the cheek. "Girl, we are going to have so much fun!"

CHAPTER TWO
Winsley

IT'S THE NIGHT BEFORE MY FIRST DAY ON SET and the constant thump of my heart is making sleep impossible. Although I'd been nervous, this morning's casting call was a breeze compared to what I'm going through now. Thinking back, today was actually kind of fun.

When I'd walked in, the waiting area was filled with masses of other hopefuls, who were looking for their fifteen minutes of fame. By the glances I received—they weren't happy with me adding my name to the list. It was discouraging for sure, and I almost left, but I knew if I did my lifelong friend would be disappointed, so I stuck it out.

The scene was as Jennifer had said, dinner but with there was an added twist she hadn't mentioned.

I was auditioning as someone whose friend had set her up on a blind date…typical. I've lost count of how many times this has happened in my real life. *I should be perfect for this part,* I thought to myself.

Not only has Jennifer tried, but also my mom and even my dad, once.

The dates never worked out, he either didn't show up or one of my friends would call after the first ten minutes and check in, giving me an out by way of an emergency. I was convinced there were no longer any good men out in the world, and I'd finally given up on finding Mr. Right.

That pessimistic attitude paired with a bundle of nerves is what I'd approached the scene with.

I was seated at a corner booth in a restaurant built by the set department, the scrutinizing stares of the producer, director, and writer had locked on me. Normally, an extra in a film wouldn't need an official audition but this was a small speaking part, which meant all the focus was on me and my missing *blind date*

Several times action had been called and each time the seat across from me remained empty. My cheeks were heated the entire time, both from embarrassment and anger at being alone. It was the second time that day I'd considered leaving, and I should have because with only ten minutes left in the hour, and the whole entire scene at risk of being cut, he walked in.

His casual stroll said a lot about him as it carried his lanky body across the room. He appeared as someone who didn't have a care in the world and thought of only himself. Which had been clear when he was reveling in the hushed gasps from the women on set, offering them winks and a crooked smile as he passed by.

It wasn't enough he was late, but playing the crowd and wasting more of my precious time made my blood boil. I wasn't shy about making it known in the death stare I had pinned on him.

When he did finally take his seat, he'd

turned that same crooked smile on me and introduced himself as Rook.

His name was familiar but I wasn't sure where I remembered it from, and right now there was no time to think about it because the director's assistant was shouting for quiet on the set.

Our lines were very few and didn't really start until midway through the entire scene, but the crew mentioned there'd be multiple camera setups and we should always be in character because they would be switching between the dining room and kitchen. We wouldn't know if we were in the shot or not until after film editing. This had sent my nerves until a flurry.

When we weren't saying our lines, we'd been instructed to make small talk because when the shots were on the dining room, we'd be the main couple in the backdrop. Although, no one could hear us, they'd wanted it to look authentic.

Whether we were having the greatest or the worst first date ever didn't matter, if it looked like we were on a first date.

Authentic is what I'd given them. I'd been

both hurt and more than irritated when he'd made me wait so long, as I would be waiting for a blind date. The fear of being stood up; the not knowing if you'd hit if off, all those things would be running through my mind in the real world could be applied here.

When he finally had shown up, and he'd taken the seat next to me, Rook wasted no time flipping that switch and slipping into character. His cocky attitude gone, he was now Jackson the apologetic, tattooed single dad who had his first night out without the kids after an ugly divorce.

How was it possible, the last ten minutes of the casting call he swooped in, shared lines with me, and got us both roles as extras on the film?

It's clear he's good at what he does.

I'm glad I got through it without passing out; a grand achievement for someone who's afraid of large crowds, and public speaking. I know I should be celebrating, in fact Rook had offered taking me out to do just that, but I'd declined.

He's a nice enough guy; maybe even attractive with his lean stature, and hint of tats peeking out rolled-up sleeves, but he's not my type and he's not Preston. Not even close.

Logically thinking, my chances with Preston are pretty much nonexistent, but like a girl with a high school crush, fantasizing one day we could be a couple is what's gotten me this far through the process. "Just three more hours and you'll be wiping the drool off your lip as you eye fuck the sexiest man alive. This time, in person," I tell myself, fluffing my pillow and turning on my side.

If I can get through tomorrow with even a lingering glance at the man who I'd let plant a seed in me for the Prestons of tomorrow, my life will be complete. For now, if I don't get some sleep, they'll surely escort me off the set because no one wants to see this face without a full night of rest—including myself.

Closing my eyes, it's only a matter of moments before complete darkness consumes me and I'm dreaming of a life with the man of my dreams, anywhere but here.

CHAPTER THREE
Winsley

THERE'S A WAIL IN THE DISTANCE. DISORIENTED and thinking it's the alarm, I pound the screen of my phone, but the sound doesn't stop—it gets louder. "Dammit," I mutter. It can't possibly be six in the morning; I just got to sleep. Shoving my phone from its place on the nightstand. It comes free from the charging cord and lands on the wood floor with a loud thud. I drop my head back to the pillow and cover my ears on either side, protecting them from what I now realize is an ambulance just outside my window.

My apartment is on the third floor, but the walls are paper-thin and pretty much every noise is unmistakable. I'll admit, I don't live in the best part of town. Even with Jennifer's help, it's been a struggle staying on my feet. The cost of living in LA is ten times what it would have been in Podunk, Nebraska, which is where I'm from. That means counting every penny and living in this ratty one-bedroom studio.

Turning over, I swipe my phone up off the floor and check the time. "Seven-thirty!" I shout, throwing the covers off my legs.

In a matter of minutes, I'm in the shower scrubbing my face and all my body parts like my life is on fast forward. There's no time for shaving or washing my hair and it kills me because what was supposed to be one of the best days of my life is already starting off as one of the worst.

I step out into the steamed room, quickly drying off then wipe the mirror down. The face staring back at me has puffy eyes, blotchy skin, and a messy bun on top my head dripping droplets of water on my shoulders. I can't decide if I should call Jennifer and cancel or cry. Neither is what I want. If I cancel, I'll probably never get the chance of meeting the man of my dreams again and if I cry, I'll just get puffier.

Instead, I pull in a deep breath, place my hands on either side of the sink, and pep myself up as best I can. "You can do this. You're Winsley fucking Starling. Bold and beautiful. If Preston Pace doesn't give the true you a second glance, it's his loss. Not yours."

It's stupid but true. His days are filled with beautiful, ageless women he could, and probably does, have with a snap of his fingers. Even if they are good people, I suspect the only thing they've ever done for themselves is swipe their own card at a coffee shop or a department store. If he wants someone real, like—living on the brink of poverty real—with an imperfection or two, then I'm his girl. Otherwise, I'll just go on with my life as if none of this ever happened.

After slipping on my bra and panties, I put a leg in my favorite pair of ripped jeans and hop around looking for a shirt. There are only two clean ones left in the closet. One is a T-shirt with the face of a cat wearing a Christmas hat on it, and the other is a spaghetti-strapped, burgundy tank top. It's obvious which one I should choose, but in times like these—when my personality is screaming for the reins—it's not an easy decision.

I tap a finger on my chin and look back and forth between the two. Settling on the logical choice, I grab the tank top and a pair of nude open-toed heels. Being true to myself doesn't mean throwing my chances away before I even meet the guy.

Once everything is tucked and fastened, I take one last check in the mirror. It's not high-end designer clothing, but it also doesn't matter because there's a good chance they'll put me in something different when I get there. I step out of view and it's a moment before I realize what I've forgotten. I glance back in the mirror. My hair still sits atop my head in a tangled mess. More time has gotten away from me and there's nothing I can do about it now. "The *I've been sleeping for days look* will have to do," I tell myself before swiping the car keys from the counter and stepping out the door.

CHAPTER FOUR

T HE RUSTLE OF COVERS, AND EXPOSED BARE ass, remind me of the guest in my bed. She means nothing to me. Just a one-night stand who's one hell of a fuck and is now lingering in my personal space.

Bringing them home is not something I do often, especially on the day we start shooting a new film I'm starring in, but this is the last shoot I'm doing in the US. The next three months we're in Canada and the schedule is aggressive. It's not like there won't be opportunities, it's more about the choice. My tastes are very specific and finding what I want is not always easy.

Garret did me a solid getting this one. She's fit and curvy in all the right places and last night had no problems doing what she was told—mostly—but her hour is now up. In fact, it was up four hours ago.

She yelps when my palm connects with her ass cheek.

"Time for you to go," I tell her, tucking my hands behind my head and leaning back against the pillow.

Turning over, her tits fall out of the sheets when she props up her head. She gives me a once over with a seductive gaze. "I thought you said I could come on set with you today."

Her whine grates on my nerves. "Not today."

"Are you sure I can't change your mind?" she asks, lowering a hand over my dick.

I catch her wrist and toss her arm back to her side. "Yes, I'm sure. Now get up, get dressed, and get out."

On a huff, she tosses the covers back and hops off the bed. "Has any one ever told you you're an asshole?"

"Ever, yes. Today, you're the first, but I'm certain you won't be the last," I counter.

My reply only provokes her frustration and

she briskly yanks up the delicate material of her panties, almost falling over in the process. It's a sight for sure, watching her hurried pace as she swipes her clothes off the floor and heads through the door, slamming it against the frame—naked tits and all.

Knowing I'll never call her again is both a sense of relief and remorse, because with a little training she would have been the perfect submissive. That pouty lip almost got me hard. I'd debated on binding her hands and showing her exactly what she could do with those lips but when she reached for me, I shut down cold.

Finding a woman who's supportive of my unique tastes and understands in the bedroom, I call the shots has been challenging. There's never been one who's checked all the boxes. They're either good at listening and doing what I say, but don't have an ounce of backbone in their body. Or they're so defiant my arm tires from punishments. "There's someone out there, I can feel it," I mutter, dropping my feet over the edge of the bed and heading toward the shower.

I lather vigorously, scrubbing her scent from my body, then step under the spray and rinse away last night's activities. It's refreshing both physically and mentally. She's in the past and someone new is on the horizon. Today is a going to be a good day.

Once I'm toweled off and back in my bedroom, I stretch the muscles in my arms and legs, prepping for some time on the floor with crunches and push-ups, and then a few quick reps on the chin-up bar fastened in the doorway.

The tightness in my arms and abs is invigorating. It's been awhile since I've spent any time on the mat, mostly it's a treadmill or weights, but today I'm running a bit late so an in-home workout it is. Something is better than nothing.

Next the chin-up bar.

Just when I'm pulling myself up and over for the final count, there's a quick knock at the door. Whoever it is, doesn't wait until I'm planted on the floor and covered in a towel, instead they walk right in.

I can't see them so depending on where they enter from, they're either getting a full view of my ass or a close-up of my dick. Both of which are equally impressive.

"Good, you're getting your workout in," he says, slapping my ass as he passes by.

It's Garret Scott, my agent. I drop from the bar and turn on him with arms flexed, prepared to lay him out. "How many fucking times have I told you not to do that?"

"What?" he asks.

"Don't play innocent with me, Garret," I bark, stalking toward him. "Coming in without permission. And for fuck's sake, it should go without saying, touching my ass."

He shrugs in response as if he's not being threatened by a man three times his size. "No need to get all bent out of shape about it, man. Perfectly harmless gesture."

"Don't do it again," I warn.

"Noted," he mumbles, dropping into the chair by the window.

Stepping into a pair of gray sweats and snatching a bottle of water from the nightstand, I lean against the doorframe. "Want to tell me what you're doing here anyway?"

He shifts in the seat and looks everywhere but at me.

"Garret?"

Glancing nervously at me, he says, "You told me I should let you know when Rook was back."

It takes a moment for his words to sink in but when they do, I'm livid. "That motherfucker!" I shout, squeezing the bottle in my hand, water goes everywhere.

Rook has been nothing but a deceitful bastard since I first met him on the set of *Brothers Reunited*.

It was a high-action military film. The plot was, as the title implies, about long-lost brothers who'd went off to war in separate armed forces divisions. Each had been injured while serving their country and they'd reconnected once they returned home.

You could say we played our parts very well, if our parts were about siblings who fought all the time.

He was always late and occasionally drunk, which resulted in forgotten lines, disrespect for the director, producers, and anyone he met for that matter.

Early on I confronted him, but even a black eye and a bloody lip didn't stop his reckless behavior. The last night of shooting, we found him passed out on a prop made up to look like a bed. It was hours before he was sober again and twenty-five takes before the film finally completed.

Rook was escorted off the premises right after—ordered never to return.

It makes me wonder why he's back now. "Where'd you see him?"

"He was on set yesterday, when they were running through placements and lines of all the extras. He's not playing an official role, Preston. He's an extra."

This surprises me. Someone of his stature, who always needs the spotlight on him, is taking a place in the background. Not possible. He has a plan, an ulterior motive of sorts, and if we don't find out what it is, there's a chance this film will be at risk for losing millions as well.

Marketed as my comeback after a difficult breakup, there will be a lot of focus on this movie, and me. There's no way I'm going to let someone else fuck this up and risk the chance at a golden statue perched on my mantle.

"We need to get down there early. I'm all up

for a confrontation this morning," I say, heading toward my clothes closet.

"Ahem."

Now what? I think. "He deserves what he gets, I'm not holding back this time." When Garret doesn't respond, I turn and find his judgmental stare on me. It's no surprise why. Working out after a shower is not the order in which things should be done. Collecting my clothes, I head back into the bathroom. "Give me five minutes," I toss over my shoulder before shutting the door behind me.

True to my word, I'm out in five and shortly after we're stepping out the double doors of the building I live in. There's a driver waiting for us with the rear door of the limousine open.

My control is hanging on by a thread right now. Just thinking about being in the same room with a rat such as Rook makes my nerves twitch. He's put one too many nails in his coffin and if he's not careful I'll seal it shut.

CHAPTER FIVE

Preston

THE PLACE WE'LL BE FILMING IN IS AN abandoned factory in a brick building across town, and the aesthetics are from an era when craftsmanship meant something. The perfect backdrop for the restaurant where I'll be taking an on-screen cooking lesson from the female lead, Gina. She's playing Juliette, a French chef.

This is not a part I would have taken normally. Most of what I've done has been action, jumping out of helicopters, or being in a high-speed car chase, those are the parts I like playing. This time I'm a wealthy bachelor, who has trouble keeping it in his pants until Juliette catches my eye. The entire story line has been described as a chick flick.

We pull into the entrance and stop at the lowered gate arm, where a security guard approaches the driver window. He requests our chauffer's credentials while another guard walks around the long black car with a mirror beneath. Both are an inconvenience but a necessary precaution and something I'd never protest. There's been one too many bomb threats.

Once cleared, we're directed to the parking area and I'm pleased to find it empty. That means we're here early and he'll not suspect a thing. "Is there anything else I should know before he gets here?" I ask flatly.

"Nah, he's the same scrawny jackass as the last time you saw him. I feel bad for the hot blonde they've paired him with. Although, when he was fifty minutes late, she gave him crossed arms and a death stare for days. I don't think she has a problem seeing right through him."

The image of him and a blonde reminds me of Tinka. There was a time, although brief, when they were a thing. It didn't last because once he'd shown the true side of himself; she was the one who ended up with a black eye. It was an accident, he'd swung at another man in a drunken fight and hit her by mistake, but it was the last straw, and she'd left. Yet another reason our lives would be easier if he was in another town, in another state, or even better, another country. "You know it's only a matter of time before he does something stupid," I tell Garret.

"I know."

"Well, you're the agent, why don't you do something about it?" He shakes his head as though it's not his problem and it pisses me off. "You've always told me you can work miracles. I guess this is just not one of them." Those are the last words I leave him with before reaching for the door handle and stepping from the car, not even waiting for the driver.

Thinking about what I expect the reaction on Garret's face looks like at the challenge I just laid on him, tips my lips up in a grin. He'll take this seriously. He's a good guy just sometimes with his lack of backbone he needs a push. It does make me wonder if I should get a new agent, but then I check my lineup of movies and decide he's good for something.

Once I reach the building, and step inside, the room is pitch-black. It's so dark I can't even see my hand in front of my face, and it forces me to fumble around until I find a light switch on the wall. When the switch is flipped the unexpected happens, an entire city comes to life. From a barbershop to a bank and even a thrift store—the level of detail is almost uncanny—the stagehands have outdone themselves.

I knew the budget would be large, but there was never a number put on paper and I expect this is why. What moviegoers don't realize is how much work goes into making sure every detail is just right. From the etching of a storefront window to the red, white, and blue barber pole perched just above the door; the researchers, designers, and artists put in a lot of hours making it look this good.

The first place I'm headed is Le'Miserie where we'll be stationed for the next couple of days, depending on how quickly we can get through this part of the script.

Garret stalks up behind me. "It feels like we're lost in a ghost town of what used to be downtown LA."

"Yeah, well, we don't have time for window shopping."

We enter the restaurant, perusing the place as though we're high-end chefs considering more real estate for our chain. Cooking food for others has never been a dream of mine and never will be. I have people for that. It makes me wonder why I took this part.

Tinka, she's the reason.

If she were a guy, the saying would go, "She couldn't keep it in her pants," but in this case she's just a promiscuous bitch who fell on the first dick she found that wasn't mine.

"Where did they seat him?" I ask Garret, wondering where Rook's table will be.

"This one, I think," he says, pointing at a table tucked back against a wall.

Nodding I turn toward the exit. "Let's find my trailer, we can wait in there."

There are three RVs parked around the side of the warehouse, each a different size and each with a burgundy and gold nameplate perched on a stake near the door. Walking past the eighty to one hundred grand machines, I'm impressed by their size and sleek design. They're basically only used for staying in between scenes, during our twelve to fourteen-hour workdays, so over-the-top luxury isn't necessary but it is required for me anyway, and this time it appears they didn't spare any expense. I find mine at the far end. It's the largest of the three and I whistle with approval without even seeing the inside. "Nice job, man. This is definitely better than the last dump you arranged for me."

"Only the best for my man Preston."

"Don't do that," I correct.

"Do what?" he asks, reaching for the door.

I'm suddenly regretting having him tag along. There's no job for him here. His job is back at his office, where he should be lining up work for me. "Don't be a kiss ass. It's not your style and isn't something I need right now."

"Got it. No ass kissing," he replies with a thumbs-up and showing a little too many teeth.

He opens the door and waves me in. Shaking my head, I shove him like a brother would a sibling as I pass by. His surprised, *fuck, I'm going to fall* look, is classic as he stumbles a few steps before regaining his balance—laughing it off when he steps inside.

The interior is straight out of a rich and famous playbook. Nothing about this massive vehicle is what the average person could ever afford in their lifetime.

Marble tile floors and granite countertops give the interior a luxurious feel, while the sleek leather, fireplace, and massive seventy-five-inch TV invite you in for a beer and good football game. It's not as nice as my apartment but it'll do while we're on set.

Right now though I'm not interested in a tour, I'm more concerned with knowing where Rook is lurking. He's nearby; I can feel it. Pacing from the small kitchen to the window and back, I wait.

It hasn't been ten minutes before makeup artists, stylists, and other essential personnel begin flooding the area. They're followed by the cameramen and catering crew, each heading to their designated areas, where they prep for the onslaught of talent expected to arrive later.

Unbeknownst to them, the only talent they should be concerned with is already here. "This isn't about you, my man," I mutter to myself.

"This is about making sure that piece of shit is booted the fuck out of here."

"Did you see this refrigerator? It's full of food," Garret asks excitedly.

"Your point?"

"They must've planned on you cooking a real meal," he chuckles.

I'd never really given it much thought, but his comment is not too far from the truth. The cooking lesson, it makes perfect sense. Using prop food would take away from the realism of the scene and that's how you lose money. Details count, even if it means learning how to cook a French entrée. Otherwise a single post on social media, from a fan who picks apart every detail, could send any potential earnings straight into a tailspin.

"He's here," Garret whispers.

Looking through the glass of the RV, I narrow my eyes on the snake walking through the parking lot. "What is he doing here early, turning over a new leaf? We're not starting at least for another…" I check my watch. "…twenty minutes. Fuck, there's no time now."

Just as the words leave my mouth, there's a

knock at the door. I take a moment, preparing the words I'm going to shout at him, and when I'm ready, I take a deep breath and pull the door open. "You son of a bitch!" But the person standing there is not him. It's Teresa, my stylist and movie makeup artist.

The smile melts from her face like ice cream on a hot day. "Is this a bad time, Mr. Preston?"

I glance around her at the space between my RV and the next. There's no sign of him, but the hairs on my arm are still standing on end, so I know he's nearby. Without a word or giving it a second thought, I grab her arm and pull her in.

She yelps, stumbling a bit, and almost spilling the contents of her carry bag on the floor, but I catch her just in time. "Umm…"

"Shhh." I place a finger over my lips, waiting for another knock at the door. When there isn't one, I relax a little and show her to the kitchen island. "You can set up over there."

"Yes, sir." she responds demurely.

I pull up a barstool while she organizes what she needs to make me look like Andrew Smith, the character I'll be playing. "Garret, make yourself useful and go find Rook. You can keep me posted on his whereabouts via text. He's only an extra, so I don't expect they'll take too long on his prep."

"Got it. Do you want me to send wardrobe your way as well?"

I look down. Wearing jeans and a black T-shirt, I consider his offer. But then decide it's not necessary. For the cooking scene they'll have me in a navy jacket like gourmet chefs wear and that can go over my clothes. "No, just have the jacket ready."

He offers a nod then heads through the door.

Once he's gone and Teresa begins brushing my hair, you could cut the thick silence with a knife. The negativity toward me is rolling off her in waves. She's been my stylist for at least five years, but I've never seen this type of reaction from her. It was for her own safety, me pulling her in like that. What's done is done, apologizing shouldn't make much difference, but I do it anyway. "I apologize for grabbing you the way I did."

"Thank you, Mr. Pace. I realize you're in a rush, so we'll get through this as quickly as possible."

"Very well, make me unrecognizable."

The comment sets her at ease, even tipping her lips in a grin as she goes back to brushing and combing. After ten or so minutes, I've become Andrew: a millionaire with a heart of gold, pining for a single mother who's barely scraping by. If she doesn't get twenty thousand dollars by the end of the week, her dreams of ever owning a restaurant are over.

This movie is right up the alley of the network that also makes greeting cards, but with A-list celebrities and ten times the budget. You can bet I'll not be watching it. But that's nothing new, I've only watched one other of my own films, and it's because it was the last one Tinka and I did together.

A Life Lost in Neverland was the ultimate rip your heart out kind of film. It was about a young girl who, as a child, had been sexually molested by her own father and then tossed into the foster system when he died. Her rage was valid because her father wasn't the only one. Each home they moved her to it happened over and over, until the day she turned eighteen.

Tinka was the emotional unstable eighteen-year-old girl who fell in love with a twenty-something boy—me.

Neverland was essentially a metaphor for never having a place to call your own. While a life lost was her childhood innocence.

She and I were ecstatic about working on this one together. Our relationship matched the young love described in the script, minus the hardships. We knew it would be an Oscar winner.

Unfortunately, she got lost in the character and shortly after the film wrapped, she struggled to find her way back out. Add to that my afterhours fetishes and in her emotional state she'd decided I was no better than the men in the movie.

Unbeknownst to me, she eventually found someone, shall we say, less adventurous.

There was a time I loved her, and it was tough letting her go, but once she'd had another that's where I drew the line.

I don't have time for my mind to drift any farther down that rabbit hole. Instead I head toward the bathroom, intent on scrutinizing Teresa's work. When I check the mirror, there's not a hair out of place and my skin is caked flawlessly with makeup. Something needed to hide any imperfections found by harsh lights and high-definition cameras.

Not that I have any, imperfections that is.

Teresa is waiting by the door when I come back out. "Does everything look okay, Mr. Pace?"

"Perfect as always," I tell her, opening the door and guiding her through. She stiffens momentarily at my touch but eventually moves along. We head opposite directions.

There's a back entrance to the restaurant and it's where Garret is waiting. "Well, what do you know?" I ask.

"I was told he's waiting behind the main door for his grand entrance."

There was a time when he would've had a main part, but he burned his own bridges and that time is not today. If he thinks he's going to come in and make this his big comeback, he's got another thing coming. I'll see to that.

"Good luck, my man. I'll be waiting behind Jackson on camera one."

I tip my head at him and walk toward the

breakfast bar for a quick espresso and an energy bar before we get started, but when I approach the row of tables I stop midstep.

There's a woman filling her small plate with fruit. I don't know or care what she's choosing though because my attention is drawn to her womanly curves and the red cocktail dress flowing easily over each one. Her look is accentuated by blonde locks that fall in waves down her back.

I could easily see myself pounding that fine curved ass with a hand gripped tightly in that hair. My dick twitches at the thought.

When she turns and her shimmering emerald eyes meet mine, she drops her plate and a hand flies to her mouth.

Her surprise is beautiful. She's beautiful. Catching my breath and rendering me, "The King of the Big Screen," speechless. After a beat I decide I want to know who she is, and I approach her cautiously.

Her eyes widen but otherwise she stays still, almost as though she's paralyzed by my proximity.

Offering out my hand, I introduce myself,

"Preston Pace, and you are?"

She places her hand softly in mine, and I can't help but wonder what her delicate fingers would feel like wrapped around my dick.

"Winsley…Winsley Starling." Her cheeks tint excessively, as she goes on, "I can't believe I'm meeting you. I've been a huge fan since I was sixteen years old."

Her comment hits me straight in the ego. Once an age is tied to a statement, there's no easy way to look past it. "I guess my reputation precedes me."

"I imagine there are very few who don't know who you are," she says, bending to pick up her plate and the fruit from the floor.

"Here, let me help you with that."

"No, no that's okay, I've got it. We can't have *The Preston Pace* crawling around on the floor like a dog."

Her words are innocent enough, but it's a considerably different image in my mind. Instead of me it's her on all fours. And in that dress, the view would be well worth her humiliation. "You can call me Preston," I tell her, picking up a cube of watermelon and cantaloupe from the floor. "Maybe a bit of normalcy from me will give the crew something to talk about." I offer her a wink and smile.

Her eyes lift to mine. "Thank you," she says, raising her plate to me. "I'm sure you didn't come here to talk with me, so I'll leave you to it then. It was nice meeting you."

Turning on her heel, she tosses her plate in the trash and begins walking away.

I'm not sure what part she's playing, which means I don't know when I'll see her next, and she's not an opportunity I intend on passing by. I call out to her, "Winsley…"

She stops and faces me. "Yes."

"Usually everyone on set goes out for drinks after the shoot, would you like to join us?" I ask the question, but fight back the urge of leaving her with no choice and ordering her to do it.

"Preston, you're needed on set," the director's assistant calls out.

She glances toward the voice in the distance and then turns back in the direction she was headed. "I'll think about it."

Who in their right mind would tell *me* they'll

think about it? I take a step forward, intent on giving her something to think about, when my name is shouted out again.

"Preston, now."

Some days David just doesn't remember who he's talking to and with my mind on Winsley, today is not a day for a reminder other than a hard clap on the back as I pass by.

Strolling into the kitchen, I find Gina and the film crew waiting.

"Preston! It's been awhile," Gina says excitedly, moving in for a hug.

"It sure has. The last time I saw you was on the set of *Days of Never*. How've you been?" I answer, squeezing her tightly.

"Has it been that long?" she says, stepping back an arm's length. "You look great, by the way."

"As do you. In fact, I'm tempted to send all these guys packing and take you right here on this island."

She laughs. "You always were quite the charmer, but my husband…" she glances toward the row of cameramen, "…might have something to say about that."

I follow her stare and cameraman two gives me a nod. "You got married?"

"I did," she says grinning from ear to ear, while holding out her left hand. "And we have a daughter."

"That's great. Congratulations," I tell her, taking her hand in mine and examining the rock perched on her finger. My words are truly sincere, but I can't help the twinge of jealousy at her happiness. While I'm not ready for that type of commitment, I wouldn't mind having someone in my life who one day I could consider *the one*. For now, I'll relish in the fact that a longtime friend of mine is in that place. If anyone deserves it, Gina is that person. "Hey, man, had I known…" I say to Gina's husband.

"The names Braydon, and it's no problem. My wife is hot as fuck and I'm sure that thought has went through the minds of many; they've just never actually said it out loud," he says with a straight face.

I take that as he's okay with my advances—this time—but if he catches me doing it again, I can expect a reminder who he is without hesitation.

"Read you loud and clear, my man. Might I suggest she remove the ten-ton weight from her finger while she's in character? She is supposed to be a single mother who falls for the millionaire bachelor." I point a finger to my chest while emphasizing my use of the word single. It's my warning back. I don't recognize him as a regular, which makes me think he's new. I've known Gina for longer than they've been married. That fact alone gives me a leg up in this pissing match.

He's challenging me with a death stare, and I'm feeling like I just won until I glance back at Gina. She's shaking her head, discouraging him from going any farther. It knocks a peg off my ego but I'm fine with that. There's no sense in stressing her out before our scene, and I've got another cocky bastard who needs taken care of.

Gina and I move into position. A quick glance at the wealth of food on the counter raises a grin to my lips. It's all real; right down to the miniscule spices separated in small individual bowls.

The director takes a seat, just below the cameras, and calls out, "Silence on set."

"Something funny?" Gina whispers.

"I'll tell you later."

"Take one," a young stagehand says.

"And Action!" the director shouts.

"Today I'll be teaching you how to make Moules Marinières, basically mussels in white wine sauce," she says, arranging the ingredients in the order in which they'll be used.

Mussels…of course. "Ah, interesting choice," I respond, admiring the way her hands move as she places the ingredients in a pot.

"Why do you say that?" she asks distractedly, while moving busily about the kitchen.

"Aren't mussels an aphrodisiac?"

It takes a moment for the question to sink in, but when it does, she stops in her tracks. Unsure how she should respond, her tongue darts out nervously and she stumbles over her words. "T-that's um what…well, I mean it's what people say, but I don't know."

"How is it you don't know? You're a French cook, aren't you?" I fire off questions, and in three long strides I'm across the room, towering over her.

At the same time, she backs away, bumping

into a rack of pans and they rattle on the shelf. "Yes, but…"

"Are you saying you're teaching me a dish you've never tried?" I breathe out, blocking her in with hands on either side of her head.

With no place to go, she looks up through her lashes. "No, that's not what I'm saying…"

Our eyes lock and her navy stare pulls me in, telling me a story of heartache and broken relationships. The sounds and smells of a kitchen pushed to the back of my mind while placing my lips on hers, does not. "Then what *are* you saying?" I ask, leaning in closer.

"I, um, I've made them before. Lots of times," she says, while her heavy breaths warm my lips.

My lips hover over hers, teasingly. "Did you try them?"

"Yes." She breathes out, placing her hands on the rack behind her for balance.

"And, how'd they make you feel?" I ask, taunting her by wetting my lips.

"They made me…well, um…"

"Juliette! Customers are filing in, are you about done with your lesson?" the head chef asks, his tone stern as he steps in the kitchen from an office down the hall.

"Almost, Chef," she replies, quickly standing straighter and brushing out the wrinkles in her clothes. No longer affected by my advances.

"Well, hurry up, we have a special guest tonight. An acclaimed food critic from the *Times*," he growls, turning around and heading back to his hole-in-the-wall.

She looks from him to me and I know what she's going to say before she opens her mouth.

"I'm sorry, but we'll need to reschedule."

Not ready to leave, I must think of a reason to stay. "How about if I just hang out and watch you work your magic? I mean hands-on is ideally the best way to learn," I give her a once-over, "but if you don't mind me being here, I feel I can at least learn something."

"I don't know. Harrison doesn't like any distractions. And you don't seem the type who just blends into the background," she says, her eyes meeting mine.

There's something there; I feel it. Moving toward the back, I lean against the wall. "I'll watch from back here."

"Not one word?"

"Complete silence." I wink at her.

"Fine." She gives in but gives me a warning look. I run my fingers across my mouth as though it's a zipper and it makes her smile. Moving quickly, she gathers all the mussel ingredients and places them in the fridge then she wipes down the area and calls out, "Chef, I'm ready for orders now."

The next two hours seem to fly by and we're on the last order. Interestingly enough, it's for the mussel dish we were about to make. She's exhausted by now but doesn't slow her pace. It's sexy watching her in her element. Confident and in control she's not the same woman she was only moments ago. "Would you like to give me a hand with this one, since we were going to make this anyway?"

"Are you sure?"

"Get over here before I change my mind."

I move next to her and we begin. She explains every detail and the reasoning behind why each step is needed. Once complete and the pristine plate holds the masterpiece we created, she wipes the sweat from her brow, and gives me an appreciative glance. "Thanks for your help. That went much quicker with two people."

My body hasn't cooled from a couple of hours ago. If anything, watching her work has raised my heat level tenfold. The way her curves flexed beneath her clothes leaves me wanting more and I intend to take it.

She begins collecting miscellaneous items from the counter when I step behind her. "Here, let me help you." In one swift move I swipe everything off the island. Twisting her around, I lift her up, and set her right where we cooked the last meal.

Our eyes lock once again, but this time mine are demanding, knowing exactly what she needs. I lower my head, and hover over her once again. When she doesn't turn away, I take that as my cue and place my lips against hers.

The kiss is innocent at first, featherlight, while we work our way through the awkwardness that is both a first kiss and two friends from another time but once the intensity builds, we're ravishing the other.

My hands are roaming everywhere and she's pulling at my shirt.

Suddenly my concentration falters and Winsley's image pops in my mind. It's my lips on hers this time, and I'll admit it sets my body on fire. If it weren't for this kitchen island, everyone would have a front row view of just how much.

The set has gone eerily quiet and in the back of my mind I'm thinking of the death stare I must be getting from cameraman two. It doesn't discourage me though; we're both professionals and understand the success of the film would require a level of authenticity in the scene. Secretly knowing he's watching is just a bonus.

"Juliette?" a young woman's voice calls out. She steps into the kitchen and gasps at what she sees.

It stops our intimacy cold. Juliette breaks away, placing a hand to her mouth, breathing heavily. It takes her a moment before acknowledging the interruption. "Yes, Alicia?"

"Um...Chef, Monsieur Bisset would like you to visit with the patrons now."

Still sitting atop the island, Juliette's eyes meet mine. I know it's the end of our encounter and I drop a quick kiss to her lips before helping her down. "To be continued?" I ask.

Glancing at my lips, she offers a slight nod. It's a promising sign that after tonight we'll be seeing one another again. For now, I gather myself and prepare to leave. She looks over to the petite girl by the door. "We'll be right out."

"We'll?" I question.

"Come with me, it'll be fun. We're going out there to talk with the diners and find out about their experience at Le'Miserie."

I grab her around the waist. "I'd rather stay in here and finish what we started."

"Believe me, I would too, but I'm also not looking to get fired," she says, pulling away and smoothing back her hair. "How do I look?"

"Beautiful."

She swats me on the arm. "I'm sure that's not true, but thanks."

Gripping her chin between my thumb and forefinger my expression turns serious. "It is."

"Well, let's just go talk to those who want to give an honest opinion," she laughs, pulling from my grip and heads through the door.

Following closely behind I shake my head at her playfulness, but once I step through the door it's as though my feet are buried in cement.

There he is.

Lost in the character I'd somehow forgotten Rook was going to be here. Glancing in his direction I'm tempted to approach him, but I know I can't, not until the director calls cut.

"Well, are you coming?" Juliette asks, redirecting my attention with a stern expression warning me I need to stay in character.

"Yes," I reply, albeit distractedly.

With each table we visit my eyes flit to him often. He's eating and chatting it up with some girl who at this moment I can only see the back of her head. There's no sign he's seen me yet, but he will.

"Right, Andrew?" Juliette asks, pulling me from my ever-present distraction.

I answer without even knowing what the conversation is about. "Hmm, oh yes, very much."

She huffs at my reply, giving me a dirty look before turning back to the diners at the table. "I'm glad you liked it, thank you for coming." Proceeding to the next table, she's surprised when I grab her arm and lead her to Rook's instead.

"What are you doing? This isn't in the script," *Gina* whispers.

"It is now," I whisper first then raise my voice for the next line. "Let's visit this happy couple next."

She glances at the table and then at me. "You wouldn't…"

"I wouldn't, we are."

There's no time for her to challenge my decision because we're already approaching the table. Like a pro though she steps up, jumping right back into character. "How was your meal?"

When I glance at the food, I realize it's the mussels order. There's only one reason Rook would suggest those as his order for this dining scene, and it's the same reason I'd asked in the kitchen.

"Well, the salad was warm, the wine not at room temperature, and I've found two mussels which have not yet opened. My date and I are extremely disappointed in your cooking and this restaurant." Rook's face creases with frustration.

On a personal level *Gina* hates Rook as

much as I do. She knows what he'd done while filming *Brothers Reunited*, because the movie industry is a tight-knit community and right now, she's prepared to lay into him. "Now, wait a minute…"

Her spiel most likely wouldn't have strayed from the script but I touch her shoulder anyway, discouraging her from saying anything that might jeopardize the scene.

She recognizes my intention and changes her approach. "I'm sorry, sir, let me get you a fresh bottle of wine and remake your entrée."

"That won't be necessary, we're leaving." He stands, replying to Juliette but looking straight at me.

I step closer and prepare to knock the shit out of him, no longer caring if we're still filming or not. Hell, it might even be an added bonus to the entire scene if the chef in training was to lay out one of the customers, but that thought quickly fizzles when the woman sitting across from him turns.

Winsley.

I wasn't prepared for this—for her. Rook is no longer at the forefront of my mind. She's basically changed my direction entirely. I'm now more interested in what she's doing with him than finishing this scene but I know I can't, not right now. The only way to recover and not fuck up this whole entire scene is to get back to the script as quickly as possible.

"Sir, please have a seat," I tell him, but only have eyes for the goddess before me. "We apologize for any inconvenience and we'll get your meal remade as quickly as possible."

I can feel *Gina's* hard stare on me, and I know she's pissed at how everything has gone to shit, but the director hasn't called cut, so we keep going.

When leaning in and gathering Winsley's plate of untouched food, I whisper, only loud enough for her to hear, "Stay away from him, he's the kind of trouble you don't want to get involved in."

A gasp escaping perfect lips is her only reply.

I'm familiar with that reaction. It happens all the time from ladies, both young and old. While I understand it's generally a form of flattery for me; it serves no purpose. None. Words—they are what people understand.

In the case of her, by not responding, how am I supposed to know she'll heed my warning? It means asking again, which is something I don't like doing. "Understand?"

With wide eyes and parted lips, she nods.

She fucking nods. The growl in my throat urges its way up threatening escape. If she were my sub, I'd turn her over this table, lift her skirt, and punish her until she was singing her response in front of all these people. On camera or off. But she's not, which means I'd better walk away, otherwise, I might say fuck it and end up doing whatever I want.

I need to redirect my focus. I glance at Juliette and she's quick to follow my lead, picking up Rook's plate she turns toward the kitchen, I follow. "Chef Bisset will be back out shortly to address your concerns."

Chancing a glance back at him, his expression tells me he's as surprised as I am that this didn't take a different turn. Unsure what to do next; he slowly takes his seat. There will be a lot of explaining to do with the crew, but I'm not concerned because right now getting back to the girl I met earlier is my main priority.

"And Cut!" the director shouts out.

CHAPTER SIX
Winsley

"**O**H GOD, DID ANY OF THIS JUST HAPPEN?"
I ask, fanning myself with a shaky hand opposite the cameras. Every beat of my heart is charging at my ribs, threatening to jump straight from my chest. I knew when auditioning as an extra, there was a chance I'd see Preston and maybe even meet him, but my optimism isn't always on target. Today was a welcome surprise.

I'm desperate to tell Jennifer about this, she'd better be prepared for an earful later this evening.

There's a mutter of a man's voice and I suddenly remember Rook is sitting across the table. When I turn to him, he's glaring at me like someone's just kicked his favorite pet. "Well? What'd he say?" he asks, leaning in as though he's got a vested interest in my personal life.

"I'm sorry?" I question, unsure if I've missed something.

"Preston, what'd he whisper in your ear?"

Taking a moment, I let Preston's words tumble through my mind in his sexy voice. *"Stay away from him, he's the kind of trouble you don't want to get involved in."* At least I think that's right; my mind was focused on his perfect lips, strong jawline, and the intriguing pools of melted chocolate swirling in those eyes. I sigh.

"It looked to me like you agreed to something," he says flatly.

I do remember nodding like a fucking bobblehead. "I think he said stay away from you. Why do you think he would've said that? I don't remember it being in the script," I say, sitting straighter and placing a hand over my mouth. "What have I done? I could've just messed up the entire scene." Jumping up, I glance around the room, looking for anyone who I can ask. Finding the director's assistant over by the cameras in the dining room, I take a step in that direction; Rook grabs my arm.

"He was probably just kidding around or maybe they added it to his script not ours. Either way, you need to sit down until we're told we can go," he says sternly.

I glance from right to left and find everyone still sitting at their tables; all eyes are on me. Slowly I melt back into the chair, tempted to hide my head from the world.

"You really shouldn't worry about it," he murmurs.

"I don't know," I say, glancing at the kitchen doors once again. "I wouldn't want to have wasted everyone's time because I made a mistake."

He shrugs. "I've done this acting gig before, just last time it was at the Preston Pace level. What I've learned is doing a scene in one take is rare. If you make a mistake, they'll either edit it out or shoot the scene again. It's why we have directors," he says, leaning back in his chair. Relaxed and confident.

I eye him closely before it finally dawns on me. "That's where I recognize you from. You're Everett Davidson, from *Brothers Reunited*. How did I not realize this sooner?" The space between us suddenly feels awkward. Why wouldn't he have mentioned anything? That movie was a big deal. As always, my curiosity gets the best of me. "If you've been acting at Preston's level, why are you only an extra on this one?"

"It's a long story. Why don't we get a drink after we're done here, and I'll be more than happy to fill you in?"

"Are you going out with the rest of the people on set?"

"I was thinking something…a little less crowded," he confirms with a little more edge than I'm sure was intended.

Looking at the man across from me and then to the double doors of the kitchen, I'm reminded of the earlier drink invitation. My heart is skipping an erratic beat again and I can't hold in my excitement any longer. "I saw Preston over by the breakfast bar and he'd also invited me out for drinks. I was surprised by the invitation so I've yet to say yes. It's a bar, there's no reason we can't all just go together."

A flash of anger spreads over his face, and although brief, it's clear he's not happy with my admission. "Do you think that's a good idea?"

Furrowing my brows at his change in attitude, I begin second-guessing if any of this was a good idea. All my focus has been on Preston. I practically know everything about him like his birth date, the fact he's an only child, his mother's maiden name, his favorite food, and a whole bunch of other stuff but it's all from magazines and the internet.

I know nothing about Rook. Not a single web search worth of information. Which means one thing, I'll be driving myself.

I remove a napkin from my lap and place it on the table but before I stand, the director's assistant begins shouting out orders.

"The director has instructed me to release everyone for the day. They'll do a playback of this scene after lunch and determine what changes should be made before moving on. On a side note, whatever happened at table nine was not in the original script. As a reminder, improv is limited, please keep that in mind for tomorrow. Have a nice rest of your day, be back here tomorrow by 8:00 a.m."

They're sending us home. I'm even more

concerned now that I've messed up the scene. There's not much I can do about it now. As Rook said, they can always edit our part out. Anyway, I got to do what I came here for. I met Preston Pace. The reminder sends chill bumps all over my body.

Speaking of the devil, Preston's standing on the dining room side of the kitchen double doors.

His attention is on the announcement being given, and that means my eyes can roam freely. I take in every chiseled feature and every curve of his clothing from the muscles bulging beneath. The costume team did their job well. Dressed in a navy, double-breasted chef jacket and a pair of formfitting jeans, he stands tall and confident. If I saw him on the street, I'm not sure I'd recognize him as the celebrity he is.

A hot, gourmet chef—maybe.

"Sounds like we're done for the day," Rook says.

I nod in response, but otherwise ignore him as I watch the man I've fantasized about since he first became a star in his early teens. My hands shake now more than ever before. "Pull it together, Winsley," I murmur, hoping it will calm the anxiety playing havoc on my nerves, but it's no use, even at this distance I'm nervous as hell.

His face is expressionless and focused elsewhere until—it isn't.

I take a chance and smile at him, but he doesn't return my friendly gesture, instead after glancing between Rook and me, his gorgeous features morph into a disapproving stare. That one small action cuts straight to my heart.

My idea of this day appeared way different in my mind than what is happening at this very moment.

There's some history between Preston and Rook, and it seems the reason I'm getting the stink eye. Well, what Mr. Pace doesn't know is, I'm up for a challenge. Grabbing Rook's hand, I tug firmly, encouraging him from his seat. "Take me someplace to eat."

He offers no resistance and is off his feet, placing his hand in the middle of my back, directing me hurriedly toward the exit.

Glancing back, I see Preston drop his arms and move toward us, but he doesn't get halfway through the room before he's stopped by someone—an incredibly attractive woman. It makes my decision to leave with Rook all that much more necessary.

Lunch is as good a way as any to get the hell out of here and get my mind off him. Even if it is with the cockiest bastard I've ever met.

CHAPTER SEVEN
Winsley

Rook and I settle into a booth inside a nearby café. It's filled with both celebrities and regular people just like me. The latter secretly, although obviously, snapping selfies with a celebrity or two in the background.

It wasn't the case when we entered though. Something odd had happened. Instead of batting eyes and audible sighs the room went silent, in fact, some people even looked away. Rook doesn't seem to let it bother him though. He stood taller and with even more confidence, something I didn't think was possible; he led to where we're sitting now.

A waitress approaches. She's not like everyone else in this place, giving us the cold shoulder. No, her grin splits her face in half, and she appears genuinely excited to wait on us. "What can I get you?"

We both take a quick review of the menu and settle on grilled chicken salads.

After our orders have been taken and the room has come alive with chatter again, I lean in. "Is this how it always is for you?"

"Unfortunately, it is," he says shifting in his seat.

It's not a reaction I'd expect coming from him. I mean, I've not known him longer than forty-eight hours, but from what I do know, unease is not something he must feel normally. "Are you uncomfortable, should we just head back and eat what the caterers brought?" My intentions are good but questioning his weakness is a mistake.

"Is that what you want? Is sitting here with me embarrassing for you? If it is then just leave, but I'm not giving these assholes the satisfaction."

Turning ten shades of red, I'm not sure I can backpedal my way out of this, but I try. "I'm not embarrassed being here with you. In fact, fuck them." I add that last part a little louder so everyone around us can hear before raising my empty water glass. "I'm staying too."

It earns me a chuckle and a clink of his glass. "That's my girl." His actions lessen the discomfort of the entire situation.

"So you said you had a story to tell?" I ask, taking a bite of salad.

"I do, but why don't we start with you first?" His stare is inquisitive as he sets his fork down on his plate.

"Me?" I laugh. "I've nothing interesting to say about me."

He leans in and reaches for my hand, "Oh come on, a beautiful girl like you. There must be something you can tell me about yourself. How long you've lived in LA and what do you think of it?"

I'm starving and have only gotten one bite of food in me but set my fork down as well, because this will take some time. "I've lived in LA for about thirteen years. What do I think of it? Well, it's expensive as hell. Since my parents died it's been a struggle living on my own. I have a little bit of money left, but I'm trying to make it last by living in some run-down apartment on the east side."

He chuckles.

"What?"

"You must really be struggling if you're living on the east side. I have some friends over that way. What building do you live in?" His tone is still lighthearted.

My hands fidget. And I consider changing the subject. I don't know him well enough to be giving out too many personal details but then again, we're on the same film, and they must've vetted these people in some way.

Recognizing my nervousness, he places his hand on mine. "Don't worry, its not like I'm asking to move in or anything. And I'm certainly not a serial killer. It's just I have some friends over there, and I'd be curious to know if it was in the same building. Maybe we could meet up again sometime."

His last comment makes me laugh. "You're right, just being careful because you never know."

"You never know." There's an edge in his tone now.

I shrug it off and begin spewing out more details than I should. "It's the four-story brick building next to the old flour factory."

"Hmm." He raises a hand to his chin and taps his lips with a finger.

While he's distracted, I sneak a peek at his tattoo. It's a hook, like something you'd find in a meat locker. Perched just in the middle of the arch is a firefly. It's unusual. I can't imagine it's meaning, other than it looks like something from a fairy tale. Which I doubt would be on someone like him.

"Yes." His finger points at me sharply. "I know the one. My friend, Lance, lived in that building." When his expression morphs into one of disgust its clear he's referring to the right place. "You live there?"

Just as I'm about to answer, gasps and a low rumble of consistent chatter begins. Every other word out of their mouths is Preston.

Unsure what's going on, I lift my eyes to Rook but he's not looking at me. Following his gaze, I see Preston pushing open the door and stepping inside.

He looks around briefly before his sights

focus on Rook. His presence is crackling with so much irritation it follows him into the room, putting everyone on edge. The fact he's even here is surprising, but it's nothing compared to what he does next. "Everyone, out!"

My mouth drops open. Did he just order an entire restaurant full of people to leave?

People scurry from the building, no questions asked.

Witnessing that kind of power is surreal. Empty tables and plates filled with food now deserted because some bastard thinks he has a right to commandeer an entire place for himself.

He stops a waitress on her way out. "Here," he hands her a stack of bills, "this should more than cover everyone's food and their inconvenience."

"Yes, sir. Thank you, Mr. Pace," she says, lingering on a long sigh before she recognizes his disinterest and joins the rest of the patrons outside. Where they all stand on the opposite side, peering through the window, and watching how this is going to play out.

I've loved this man from afar for I don't know how long. Had I known he was such a dick, I probably wouldn't have given him a second thought. Although that's not entirely true, because looking at him right now, some point between the warehouse and here he's removed the chef's jacket and is now sporting is a formfitting T-shirt.

I stand, intent on confronting the man whom I'd now rather not even be in the same room with. Taking a step, I point a finger and begin my verbal assault. "How dare you…"

Rook yanks at my arm. "Have a seat. We're not leaving."

"I wasn't going to leave, I was…"

"Sit," he orders.

Not him too. The testosterone levels in this small café just shot up tenfold.

Still standing, I glance between them. Preston's eyes are on Rook's hand covering my wrist, and Rook's grin is morphing into some sort of mischievous smile. This is some sort of celebrity pissing match.

Neither of them knows me, but it looks as though they're about to kill the other over me.

When I decide I'm no longer interested in this conversation, I try to break free from Rook's grip—he squeezes tighter. "Let go…" I tell him, panic raising my voice an octave higher.

"Just have a seat. It seems the three of us are having a talk," he says, pulling me down onto the chair next to him and wrapping his arm around my shoulder.

Every part of me is shaking. At this point in time, I'm not sure who I should be more afraid of.

"Let her go, Rook. This is between you and me."

"No can do, man. I saw the way you were looking at her and then to find out you invited her out for drinks. Tsk tsk. Just remember, I know your dirty little secrets. I think she'll be a lot safer here with me."

Preston's step falters at Rook's comment but he recovers quickly, and he closes in on us. "Whatever you think you know about me is bullshit."

The grip around my wrist tightens as the level of emotion rises. I try to pull away. "Please just let me go." My pleas are ignored.

"I don't know, man, Tinka was pretty adamant about how you like things done."

"You motherfucker!" Preston shouts, stalking toward the table.

Rook releases me, preparing to defend himself and I use it as a chance to break free, but it's only for a moment because Preston reaches out and grabs my arm.

When our skin connects it's electrifying, sending a jolt through my entire system. My instincts are telling me to slip from his grasp and run, but my body is leaning in, melting in his arms.

"Everything okay in here, Mr. Pace?" a man asks, strolling in like he didn't just step into a celebrity fight match. His nonchalant attitude is almost comforting, like this kind of thing happens all the time. Maybe it does.

"Everything's fine, Garret. Can you take Winsley to her apartment?" I've got some things to finish up here." His stare narrows back on Rook.

"Yes, sir." the stranger replies, reaching for my arm, but I pull away.

I have no idea who this man is, in fact, I don't really know any of these men. Not well enough to leave with them, yet they each feel they can put their hands on me. "It's okay, I can drive myself home."

In a swift move Preston pulls me to his chest. It's not an intimate move. In fact, I crash against him like a rag doll. And what he says next leaves no room for debate. "You'll ride with Garret, that's not negotiable." Glancing from me to Rook and back, he adds, "On second thought, Garret take her to my penthouse, it seems she and I have some things to talk about."

CHAPTER EIGHT

 Once they're gone Rook leans back in the booth, a sick confidence exudes from the space around him. "You have a lot of nerve coming back here," I tell him.

"Last time I checked, you didn't own the production company and unless I'm mistaken, the law doesn't prevent me from taking another job with Mercury Inc."

"A restraining order might."

"Do you have one?" he asks.

Neither I nor the production company has one, so I remain quiet.

"Exactly what I thought. You know what that means, right? You have no control over where I work, or what I do. Which includes that nice piece of ass Winsley."

"Stay away from her," I warn.

"Or what? Leave her in your capable hands where you can teach her to be your sex slave? I don't think in good conscience I can let that happen," he retorts.

I step in closer, a flash of panic flits over his face. "How does that differ from you drugging them and fucking limp bodies after they've passed out. At least the women I'm with are conscious and begging for it."

He pulls a phone from his pocket. "How about we call Tinka and ask her how often she begged to get fucked?"

It's the last straw for me. I'm quicker than he is, and I reach across the table, grabbing the collar of his shirt, pulling him like a rag doll across its surface.

The last time I saw him, he was in much better shape physically and would've made a worthy opponent, but years of alcohol and drugs have made his body weak and vulnerable. Now, he's losing his energy and this fight.

I raise my fist and prepare for impact, but an image of Winsley chooses this very moment to flood my mind and I hesitate.

She was scared, shaking even, but instead of feeling any remorse for causing her distress, all I can think of is how much I'd love that same reaction from her in my bed. I suspect she'd say my chances of that are a cold day in hell, but I'm confident I can convince her otherwise.

Unfortunately, my daydream has put me in a position where Rook is no longer the victim. He pulls away and lays a hard uppercut on my chin before raising his hand for another. Luckily, I'm able to thwart his next attempt because his fist was headed straight for my nose, and breaking it would mean a delay in filming.

He continues his swings, making a few solid hits against my chest and side, but they have no effect on me and this game is no longer interesting. Instead of knocking him on his ass, I grab his wrists, twist them behind his back, and buckle his knees until he's lying flat on the ground.

Cheers and clapping sound from outside. When I glance up, I find a larger crowd has gathered on the other side of the window, snapping pictures, and recording the entire thing. One even gives me a thumbs-up.

"Fuck. We've got a much bigger audience now."

Rook cranes his neck, glancing in the direction of the window, and then dropping his forehead to the floor. "You're a son of a bitch. This is just one more thing the media will have a field day with."

Sirens wail in the distance and their timing couldn't be more perfect, or so I thought.

He lets out a deep breath and flips onto his side, elbowing me in the groin.

I double over.

"You'd better watch your back," he says, kicking me in the stomach with the pointed toe of his shoe before heading toward the door.

From my position on the floor, I see the crowd part as he walks out. No one tries to stop him, instead most just stand there in awe while others come rushing in to see if I'm okay. I'm thankful for those who offer help, but really, I just want to get the fuck out of here. He'd given me a warning but I'm not returning the favor. He'll get his, and I plan on being the one who delivers it.

The red and blue lights flash a steady pace outside, but I'd rather not deal with the police.

Glancing around, I look for another exit. There's no hiding from this, it was probably all over the web after the first punch was thrown, but I'm not in the mood for hours of questions when they'll only send me home anyway.

"This way," the waitress I'd handed the money to earlier says. "We can head through the kitchen into the back alley." Like a godsend she leads me away from the masses of people who've now filled the small dining area.

When I step into the alley, my driver is waiting near the rear door of the limo, opening it when I approach. I'm not sure how he knew where to meet me because I hadn't told him.

Once we roll out onto the interstate, I tap out a quick text to Garret.

Got into it with Rook.

Cops are here. I snuck out the back

I'll be there shortly

The traffic is still typical LA bumper-to-bumper on the way home. Everyone is heading back to work after lunch, and it makes me think of where I should be. It's unclear if there will be any more work on the film today. I hadn't stayed long enough for any of the announcements after I'd followed Rook and Winsley out when they left for lunch, which means I don't know what is going on back at the warehouse.

There's been no reply to my earlier text. I decide to call Garret.

His voice permeates the interior of the vehicle through the speakerphone. "It's all over the internet. I've got directors and producers on one line and the cops on the other. What would you like me to tell them?"

"I'll tell you about it when I get there. For now, find out if they're rescheduling today's shoot. And you can give the cops my address; we can explain everything when I get there. Oh and, Garret…"

"Yeah?"

"…how's she doing?"

"As well as any woman would be in a strange man's penthouse—even yours—she wants to go home. You might as well tell me now where you keep your handcuffs because if you're not here in the next five minutes, it'll be the only way I'll be able to keep her here."

There should be humor in his tone. Something. Anything that would say he's kidding. But I get nothing. He wouldn't know a way around a woman's body if she was sitting on his face, and I'm most certainly not telling him where my cuffs are, or any toys for that matter. By now he must know I also don't share my women. If he tapped her with that pencil dick of his, she might as well leave because it would be over before it ever got started.

Maybe I'm jumping the gun; she's not my woman, but I have a feeling it's only a matter of time.

"Just try and keep her calm. Do you think you can do that?" I ask.

"Sure man," he replies.

Disconnecting the phone, I slip it back in my pocket and glance out the window. I notice the traffic around us letting up and I call out to the driver, "Jake, can you kick it up?"

"Yes, sir," he replies, and the long car jolts forward.

CHAPTER NINE
Tinka

THE VIDEO IS GRAINY AND SENT ANONYMOUSLY to my phone. This is the fifteenth time I've watched it, yet I still have no idea who the girl is or why she's there with Rook, and why my Preston is letting her lean into him like that.

Even though my past with both of these guys has been riddled with heartache and physical pain, it doesn't mean I'm ready to watch them hook up or fight over some new piece of trash, who for some reason thinks she deserves a place in their lives.

I squeeze the phone, wishing I were stronger and could feel it breaking. Sure, I could smash it against the wall, but I don't think I'd find it nearly as satisfying as using my own hands.

Instead, I settle for dropping it facedown on the café table outside the very restaurant they were at earlier.

I'm not sure why I'm here, whether it's hoping he'll come back, or if she will, alone.

Finding out who she is would be as simple as asking Rook, but right now I'm not prepared to answer all the questions he'd ask. And if I held back, he would surely come to his own conclusion, which I expect would be right on target.

There is no one, and I mean no one, who will want any part of what I have planned. Which is okay because I won't need any help.

A waitress approaches the table. "What can I get for you?"

"Bring me a gin and tonic…" I tell her, but pause briefly to glance toward the XJ sedan across the street with my driver in it, and add, "make it a double."

"Yes, ma'am," the woman says, drifting back into the café.

The large black floppy hat atop my head and sunglasses too big for my face have done their job well, otherwise, I'd be swarmed by fans. The tabloids can say whatever they want about me and how this breakup has ruined my career, but none of it's true. Only one film on my docket, pfft, my agent can name off at least five upcoming films and a limited television series. I'm not worried.

While I wait for my drink, I lift my phone from the table and watch the video once again, pausing on a shot of her face then expanding the image with my fingers, I stare at it for the longest time. "Who are you?" I ask the screen, imagining she'll magically tell me. Instead something even better happens.

"Hey, that's the girl who was here earlier," the waitress says, setting my drink down on the table.

I almost give myself whiplash twisting my head around. Tipping my sunglasses, down I pin a hard stare on her. "You were here?"

"Sure was," she says, holding a big round serving tray to her chest. "I actually waited on them, her and Rook."

His name rolls off her tongue like smoke from a cigar. I throw up a little in my throat. There's no way he'd ever be interested in a waitress, especially one as plain as her. Nevertheless, she may have information I need. "He's a dream, isn't he?"

"God, yes. He's on my top ten list of celebrities for sure," she says, fanning herself.

Intrigued I ask, "Oh? Top ten?" Instantly regretting the question as soon as it's asked because she laughs and pulls up the seat next to me. It's a move of someone who has a story to tell. One I don't expect the time or patience for, and by the looks of her it'll be a long one.

Once she starts, she doesn't stop. "Everyone has one, you know that list of celebrities you'd like to…well, you know. As I said, it's usually ten but there are so many hotties my list is double if not more. Rook's not my number one, but he's probably top five. His hard edge and tattoos make my…"

I can't bring myself to listen any further. "You're sure you saw this girl?" I point at the screen of my phone, cutting her off before she says something vulgar and puts an image in my mind of something I could never unsee.

"Yep, that's her. I was only at the table for a couple of minutes before the whole fight scene happened." She leans in, glancing around. "I know I shouldn't say this because fighting is never a good thing, but damn, it was so hot."

I push my glasses back up on my nose. It's mostly because of her proximity but also so I can roll my eyes at her ridiculousness. "Back to the girl. Did you by chance get her name?"

"Hmm, let me think. It was unusual and I think it started with a W. Willow…no. Wynter… no. Wendy…maybe."

"Wendy?" I ask, scrunching my face, what a horrid name. Who names their kid after a fast food place?

"No, that's not right…it was…Winsley, yeah that's it. Winsley. I told you it was unusual," she says, standing up proud that she remembered.

Unusual…if only she knew who she was talking to. "You didn't happen to catch a last name, did you?"

"No, ma'am. First name basis only." She grins.

"Okay, thank you and thank you for the drink," I tell her in a hard tone, lifting my drink, signaling goodbye, and hoping she'll get the hint we're done here.

"Would you like anything to eat? Or anything else?" she asks.

I can tell from her desperate tone she has very few friends and only wants to stay and talk, but I've got things to do, and they don't include sitting here any longer. Sucking down my drink, I pull forty dollars from my purse and set it on the table. "No, thank you."

"All right. Come see us again. Ask for Rayleen."

Lifting a hand over my shoulder, I wave her away as my short steps carry me quickly across the busy street to where my driver opens the door. I slip into the smooth leather seat and toss the floppy hat and sunglasses onto the seat next to me.

Once the driver is within hearing range, I spew out orders, "Driver, take me home, but don't take the route you did last time. It may be shorter, but it doesn't take me past his apartment complex and you should know, after driving me for five years we, always take the same route."

"Yes, Miss Tinka."

Pressing my finger on button, it raises the divider between us and I'm punching out a call to Shawn, the biggest mistake of my life. He's the director I'd had a one-night stand with. It was a huge mistake and not one I'm proud of. Drunk and disorderly is how I'd been described. Once I'd learned of Preston's fetishes I was done.

"Hey, baby, are you coming over tonight?" he says, his voice slinking through the line.

Ignoring his attempt at sexy, I get straight to the point. "Shawn, you know people, right?"

"I know a lot of people. Who are you looking for specifically?"

"Someone who can find out stuff?"

"Whatcha got?"

"There was a fight at Le Petite Café today at around lunchtime. Prior to that fight there was a girl there with Preston and Rook. Her first name Winsley and I have video. I need to know everything about her."

The line goes quiet and when he comes back on his voice is much quieter. "He said he can do it. But Tinka…"

When he says it like that, I know something else is coming and I brace myself. "Yeah?"

"You owe me, I'm thinking dinner at Vespertine."

"Once you get me the information, we'll talk." I disconnect the line just as we turn the corner of Preston's street. I drop the divider and meet the driver's eyes in the mirror. "Take it slow."

He nods and the car's pace slows to a crawl.

CHAPTER TEN

BY THE TIME I GET BACK TO THE APARTMENT, Winsley's already waited for over forty minutes and I'm afraid she'll be waiting for me at the door, ready to leave, instead she's standing at the window looking out at the view when I walk in.

My apartment is on the twentieth floor of a high-end luxury complex. I could've chosen a million-dollar mansion, or something with a yard at least, but I'm not here often enough to really care about the size of my living quarters, or lawn maintenance for that matter.

Instead I settled for a million-dollar view.

It consists of a long line of white beach that spreads from north to south as far as the eye can see. On the left and right of this building are more apartment complexes, and a hotel or two, but the money shot is the ocean waves crashing against the shore.

It's a beautiful sight, one I don't appreciate often enough and today it has an added bonus of the beauty standing on this side of the glass. I'd give half my fortune to know what she's thinking, instead I settle for pouring a couple glasses of red wine and strolling over to join her.

Lifting an arm over her shoulder, I dangle the glass in her view. "I hope you like red."

She looks at the offered red liquid, after which her eyes meet mine as she reaches for it. "Red is fine, thank you."

There's a whirlpool of emotions going on in those emerald eyes. It intrigues me and I'm curious to know more. "You look lost in thought; would you like to share?"

She tips the glass up to her lips with shaky hands, before she starts, "I was thinking, how it's possible I'm in Preston Pace's apartment, and how I'm looking out his window at one of the most amazing views I've ever seen. But now, I'm wondering if that's your line?"

"My line? If you're talking about what I might say to get you in bed, then no," I reply, taking a sip of wine and meeting her stare in the glass's reflection. "I wouldn't ask."

Darting her tongue out and across her lip, she lowers her eyes to the liquid that will eventually make this awkward situation a lot more comfortable.

Her actions make my dick twitch. I'm tempted to toss her over my shoulder and haul her in the back, but what I say next surprises even me. "Let's call it an exercise. I'm genuinely interested in finding out more about the woman who's filled my thoughts since this afternoon." That sounded a lot different in my mind. I can't give her the impression she's been the object of my obsession since this morning, and quickly add, "Also to understand why she felt it necessary to defy a recommendation I thought had been crystal clear."

Her brows crease and she asks, "Recommendation?"

"Let's not jump ahead. Why don't you tell me something about yourself, and then we can discuss what you should have done versus what you actually did."

Eyeing me cautiously, it appears as if she's considering how much information is enough, but then she hits me with something I hadn't expected. "I've never been with a man before. Does that earn me a turn in bed with the infamous Preston Pace?"

If she were any other woman her sarcasm would be grounds for a punishment, and I'd already have her ass up, pounding her from behind. But fuck, a virgin? It explains why she's nervous as hell and why my body is feeding off those nerves like they're a last meal.

I lean in, lowering my tone. "Be careful what you ask for. In case you've forgotten, you're in the king's castle."

Her eyes meet mine. What were once whirlpools of green are now an endless ocean amid the wrath of a hurricane. They're begging for calm and control. Something I'd be more than happy to give her.

"I haven't forgotten," she breathes out.

With three simple words I lose the last thread of my control. Cupping her face and forcing my lips on hers—I take what I want.

She stiffens. Surely, she's kissed before. I consider the possibility she hasn't because she seems unsure how to handle the assault on her tender mouth. If innocence had a taste, it would be her. Minty and fresh with a touch of merlot. A growl deep in my chest escapes. It boosts her confidence and her lips awkwardly sync with mine. Our tongues frantically search for the other.

Our motions grow more intense and I back her up against the window, my hands moving to her waist where I pull her against me, and my hardened dick. Suffice to say, she has been kissed before and if I have my way, it will never by anyone else again—because from this moment on—she's mine.

There's a knock at the door.

It breaks her concentration and she pulls away breathing heavily. Her swollen lips are parted slightly. Unable to resist, I lean in and bite the bottom one and suck it into my mouth, and she yelps.

There's a knock again.

"Goddammit, where is Garret?" I growl, dropping my forehead to hers.

"He said he was stepping out," she breathes back, the warm air tickling my lips and sending a shiver straight south.

In this one moment I wish I had X-ray vision because if I did and it wasn't the cops, I'd be sweeping her off her feet and carrying her to the bedroom. "It's probably the police."

"The police? Why would the police be here?" she asks, taking a step back.

"Rook and I had a discussion. More physical than verbal, unfortunately." She takes in a quick breath and places a hand over her mouth.

"Is he okay?"

That's when I notice it, the bruising around her wrist. Taking her chin between my thumb and forefinger, I tilt her head up but she doesn't meet my eyes. Hers are focused on the continuous knocking at the door. "Look at me," I command.

She does.

"He's fine, as am I, but what about you?" I retort, holding my thoughts on telling her why she never should have left with him to begin with.

"What about me?" she asks with irritation.

I take her hand in mine, stretching it out, and showing her the bruise.

She quickly covers it with her other hand. "I'm fine."

"You're not fine. I warned you to stay away from him. He's not the guy you think he is, Winsley," I explain, taking her elbow gently in my hand and leading her over to the wet bar. "Let's get you some ice."

The knock is harsher this time, and we both glance in that direction.

"I can manage with this; you'd better see who it is."

She's right. Whoever it is doesn't seem like they're going away anytime soon. I place a kiss on her forehead. "This won't take long then we can finish what we started."

She turns a bright shade of pink. It hardens my dick even more than it had when I tasted her lips, but if I'm being honest, not more than when she announced she was a virgin. The chances of finding a woman like her become less and less exceptional with each year that passes.

Stalking toward the door, I find out who's on the other side through the peephole. To my dismay it's not the police, instead it's someone I'd never expected.

"Tinka. What are you doing here?" I ask, standing in the empty space of the open door. If she finds Winsley here, the night will most certainly be ruined.

Placing her palm on my chest, she presses against me, hoping she can work her way in. I don't budge. She leaves her hand there anyway.

"When I saw you on the video, I thought I'd come by and make sure you were okay. Are you?"

"I'm fine, Tink. Now really isn't a good time," I reply, but make the mistake of glancing back into the room.

"Is there someone here?" She huffs out, "It's the woman from the video isn't it?"

Her question clarifies the exact reason she's here. It's not about me or my well-being, it's about her jealousy. Which is ironic, considering her cheating is the reason we're not still together. "That's none of your business. You made that decision when you decided you wanted another man," I tell her, using my body to close the gap between the door and its frame.

Throwing a hand on her hip, her face creases with anger. "Well, if you're not going to let me in, then I'll just send everything I know about Winsley to the tabloids," she says, ignoring the comment about her infidelity. "How do you think your fans and the media would react? I'd bet the new girl in the fucked-up anti-duo that is Preston and Rook would get her a lot of press. Maybe make her more than just an extra."

"As soon as that video went viral, I knew it wouldn't take you long to dig up something on her. But, Tink," I lower my tone so only she can hear, "you'd better be careful about divvying out threats so freely, because you never know who's watching."

This pisses her off and she shoves the door, managing to duck under my arm, and force her way inside.

I should toss her out, but the devious side of me wants her to meet Winsley. Someone her exact opposite. Down-to-earth both mentally and physically. Not pumped up with a fake only a doctor could prescribe.

Closing the door, I cross my arms and lean against it, watching from afar. The catfight is about to begin.

CHAPTER ELEVEN
Preston

WITHOUT SAYING A WORD, SHE HEADS straight for the woman who, at this point, is giving me the narrowest fuck you look I've ever been dealt.

"Hi, I'm Tinka," she introduces herself, offering Winsley her hand as if she expects it to be kissed.

"Winsley, and I know who you are," she bites back, ignoring the outstretched hand, crossing her arms instead.

The nervous girl from moments ago has suddenly morphed into a confident lioness, prepared to take out her rival. What's also a bit humorous, because she's been here for less than two hours, is she's already picking up my signature move.

Tinka saunters over to the wet bar, her back to me, but when she turns around there are two glasses in her hand. One wine and one whiskey. "Well, you have me at a disadvantage then, how do you know me?" she asks, offering Winsley a glass.

Winsley takes it without much thought.

"I read the tabloids, and I watch the news. In fact, pretty much all the news last month was about Tinka and Preston's big breakup."

The cackle coming from the bar sends a shiver up my spine and I watch my ex cautiously. I don't trust her. If she ruins whatever this is with Winsley, she'll have me to answer to me. Nevertheless, this should be good. The movie industry is Tinka's domain.

"The tabloids? Ha! The last story about Preston and me that had any truth to it was when the headlines read 'America's Favorite Couple.' The rest is just crap they write to fill the pages."

"Are you still together?" Winsley asks Tink, but her eyes are on me.

I raise a brow and shake my head no.

"No, but…" Tinka responds with a glass of whiskey just shy of her lips.

"Well then, I guess they got something else right, too," Winsley says cutting her off, and pinning her with a smug stare.

At this very moment, I'm feeling a bit proud of my new girl, but she just lit the fuse to a bomb I'm not sure I'm even ready for.

Tinka's expression morphs quickly into a hatred even I don't recognize. I take a step, but she catches me out of the corner of her eye and raises a hand, signaling she's done with that line of questioning, but what comes next is much, much worse.

"Since we're on the subject of Preston, where did you meet him?"

"I first saw him on the set of a *Taste of Yesteryear*." Winsley glances at me, and I give her a nod, encouraging her to continue. "We didn't meet until this morning."

"Well, isn't that interesting," she spits out with enough attitude to freeze hell. "You just met, yet here you are, in his apartment with swollen lips and looking a bit flushed. Did Garret hire you?"

"Careful, Tinka. Now is not the time," I warn. It's obvious where she's going with this.

"Why not, Preston? Isn't that how this works? Garret gets you a girl, you fuck her ten ways from Sunday and then you toss her aside."

Winsley's eyes snap to mine and her horrified expression says it all. Her view of me just took a nosedive from the clouds we were in only moments ago, straight into the gutter.

"That's enough!" I shout, my steps eat up the floor as I close in on her. "It's time for you to go."

"But I haven't finished my drink," she says, taking a small sip of whiskey.

"Take it with you," I growl.

When I reach her, she cranes her neck to meet my eyes and her hand rests on my chest, again. Ensuring she's perfectly in view of the woman who is probably thinking she'd rather be anywhere but here. I grip Tinka's arm and direct her to the exit.

But just as I'm about to toss her out, there's another knock at the door.

"What is this Grand Fucking Central Station?" I growl, knowing this time it is the police because even though I gave Garret strict instructions to knock, he doesn't always listen; he'd be strolling right in.

Pulling open the door I'm met by two uniformed officers.

"Preston Pace?" the younger one asks, but he doesn't wait for my answer before his eyes are on Tinka.

"Yes, I'm Preston, and this is Tinka. She was just leaving."

"Are you sure I can't stay and provide moral support?" Tinka asks, leaning in and rubbing against me.

"I'm sure," I respond, encouraging her into the hall with a hand on her back.

"One moment," the older man says. "Tinka, is it?"

"Yes," she responds inquisitively.

He offers her a tired smile. "Were you at the Le Petite Café earlier today; say at around twelve thirty?"

"She wasn't there," I answer. "The young woman you're looking for is waiting in my living room. I would prefer you limit the questions to avoid any further undue stress."

The older man looks at me with disbelief, I suspect at my answering for both. He turns to Tinka. "Is that true, Miss?"

She lets out a deep sigh. "Preston is correct. I wasn't there, I'd only seen it on the video posted all over social media."

"In that case, you may go. We may need to ask you some questions later."

On a huff she stomps through the door and across the hall to the penthouse elevator. The young detective's eyes are on her the entire time, and his focus doesn't return to the situation at hand until the elevator doors have closed.

When he turns back, the older officer and I are both staring at him.

Tinka is beautiful and she's been known to turn a head or two. Particularly mine. But in the case of this officer, it's not clear if he was doing it for safety's sake or his own personal gain. The question is never asked because I just want this over with.

"Mr. Pace, where would you like to speak?"

"We can discuss in my study. My apologies, I didn't catch your names."

They glance between one another as though

there's a secret between them. It could just be my own mind imagining it, but in my line of business, people are always trying to get close. Either with an intent to harm or because of their own disturbed obsessions. Checking all the boxes like getting their names and credentials will give me some sense of solace.

"I'm Officer Ryan," the younger man says, tapping his badge plate.

"And I'm Sergeant Galloway."

"Come on in, gentlemen."

They step into my home and wait off to side as I close the door.

"Please understand, Miss Starling has been through an ordeal today, I'd appreciate if you'd limit your questions for now. Then if you don't get what you need, I will personally escort her down to the station tomorrow."

A look passes between them before the sergeant answers, "We'll do our best, Mr. Pace."

"Very well, follow me," I say walking over to Winsley. They follow, albeit a few steps behind. Once I'm standing before her, I place another kiss on her forehead and introduce the men behind me. "The officers here wish to ask you some questions."

She lets out a long breath and leans into my arm, heating my body but this time, thankfully, I've got my dick under control.

"Hi, Winsley, I'm Sergeant Galloway and this is Officer Ryan. We understand you were at the café around lunch with Mr. Pace and a gentleman named Rook. Is that correct?"

She glances at me and I squeeze her shoulder, encouraging her to answer. "Yes, sir, I was there, but they were only talking, nothing physical."

"What was their conversation about? Do you remember?" the younger officer speaks up asking the question, eyeing me with distrust.

"Yes, Rook had his hand on my wrist tightly, and Preston was asking for him to remove it," she answers confidently, yet leaves out key parts of the conversation. Most of which I'll fill them in on later.

The older officer has taken out a notepad and is jotting things down. "Do you know Rook's last name?"

"Um, no, I'm sorry I don't. I only met him yesterday at a casting call." A shiver runs over her body vibrating against my own. I expect the day's events are beginning to take their toll.

"James Rook," I tell them.

"Pardon me?" Officer Galloway queries.

"Rook is his last name; his first name is James," I tell them, and her eyes flit to mine but all I can do is shrug. It all goes back to her not knowing the man she seemed so comfortable with is not the person she expected.

More notes are taken. Sergeant Galloway is as thorough as he can be, as he's from an older generation. Why he's not having the youngster take notes is a question I'm tempted to ask but keep my mouth shut, as it might delay their time here.

He looks up from the notes. "Okay, one last question. Did he hurt you at all?"

She looks at me, and I pull her closer, this time I'm answering because what he's done pisses me the fuck off. "When he grabbed her arm, his grip was so tight it left a bruise."

"Mind if we have a look?" he asks her.

She shakes her head no and outstretches her arm. The ice must've helped because it doesn't look as bad as it had moments ago.

"Ah, that's a pretty good bruise there, my

dear. Do you wish to press assault charges on Mr. Rook?"

She yanks her hand back in one swift move and pulls away from me. "What? Absolutely not. He made a mistake. I'll be fine. Now if you don't mind, I'd like to go home."

"Well, if you're not pressing charges then you're free to go," Sergeant Galloway says. "I really appreciate you taking the time to talk with us. Here's my card if you remember anything or if you have questions later."

Her unease is palpable, add that to her admission of wanting to go home, and it's a hit straight to the chest. "Let me show them to my office and then I'll page Jake to bring you to your car. Does that work?"

She nods lifting her eyes to mine. The ocean is still raging in those emerald orbs. Something I hope to tame in the near future, just not today.

A deep sigh tumbles out of my chest. "Can you humor me and maybe give me a verbal response, it's important to me, Winsley."

"Yes, that's fine. I'll wait here until you return."

"Good girl," I tell her, placing a kiss on the

top of her head. "I'll be right back, make yourself at home. Come on, gentlemen, I'll show you how the rich and famous live. We can talk more in my office."

CHAPTER TWELVE
Winsley

ONCE THEY LEAVE THE ROOM, I DROP ONTO the couch and relish in the fact I kissed Preston Pace. And not just some peck on the lips. I could literally feel my body melting against him. If he had picked me up and carried me off to his bedroom, I wouldn't have resisted. In fact, I'd never been more ready for a man to take my virginity than after the kiss I'd had with "The King of the Big Screen."

But when his ex walked in, it was like a bucket of ice water had been dumped on me. And Tinka is exactly as she's been described in all the media. Evil.

The way her hand lingered on his chest, and the sickening sweet way she spoke—even when spewing out attitude—wasn't lost on me. Between the time she stepped through the door and the time she'd left; it was crystal clear she's still hung up on him.

The type who would do whatever it takes to keep her hooks in him.

It's a lot of baggage. Being with him would mean dealing with her, and that's something I'm not sure I'm ready for.

Maybe I'm overthinking things. I need to take a breath, sitting here in this room is making me feel claustrophobic. Before Garret left, he'd mentioned the door locks are controlled by a code, to which he didn't give me the number. It means I'm basically trapped here until Preston gets done or Garret comes back.

Which I thought would be well before now.

"I'm not going to just sit here." I tell myself and the expensive furnishings in the room.

Standing, I walk about the living area and then the kitchen, stopping only to grab a piece of fruit off the plate in the fridge, before moving toward the hallway. It's the same way they went and while I'm not looking to barge in on their meeting, I am bored and feeling a bit mischievous by taking my own tour of his apartment.

As soon as I turn the corner, I'm disappointed to find all the doors down the hall closed. It makes peeking in even more exhilarating because I don't know which one they're in.

Taking my chances, I move to the first door. Pressing my ear against it and listening for voices. There are none so I try the knob. It's unlocked. I push it open.

Inside is a luxurious bathroom with marble floors and what appear to be nickel fixtures. It's the size of my own apartment. Stepping out, I latch the door quietly and move on to the next. This time it's on the other side of the hall and appears to be a beautiful but typical guest room.

The bed looks inviting. I'm tempted to crawl in it and nap, or finger myself until my come is all over the sheets—maybe both—but this game of door roulette has my heartbeat in a flurry and I intend to keep going.

The next three doors consist of a workout room, a sauna, and another guest room. Now, it's the last two. One must be his office and the other a master bedroom.

This time I'm taking a chance by not listening first, if he's in there I can make up some excuse about trying to find the bathroom.

As with the others, this door is not locked. I turn the handle and push my way in and instantly I'm blindsided by the very size and beauty of this room.

This is clearly his bedroom, but could be a concert hall. In awe I mindlessly step inside. Why would anyone need this much space only to sleep in? Dark pleated material is hung in swags over the windows, while the same color and pattern extend to the duvet cover on the oversized king bed. Modern patterned plush throw rugs scattered about the hardwood floors. They look soft and it draws an image in my mind of me kneeling in front of him.

The bed appears to be an oversize king sufficient for holding a man of his size, and a few others, but that's not something I want to imagine so I turn my attention to the rest of the interior. There's the typical matching dresser, armoire, and side tables, along with a love seat, but there's also something tucked in the corner on the other side.

I glance back at the door to make sure no one is coming before I stalk over to the corner to get a closer look. It resembles a dog kennel but with much thicker bars and a lot larger than the average person might have in their home. Plus, a dog large enough to fit in this would be hard to miss. No, this is something else.

Once I'm close enough to touch the bars, I notice a flash of metal. Handcuffs hanging from the top of the cage. The pink fuzzy pillow and the princess plaque on the front now make sense. My hand flies to my mouth. This is some sort of sex slave cage.

In his bedroom.

I may still have my virginity but I'm not a prude. I knew stuff like this existed, I'd just never thought I'd meet someone who was into it. What if this is what he has planned for me? It's intimidating and suddenly my lungs are pounding at the same rate of my heart as breaths come quickly.

Intent on getting out, I turn quickly but end up running straight into his strong chest.

He places his hands on my arms. "When I told you to make yourself at home, it didn't mean wandering through my home and looking through my things."

"I was looking for the bathroom," I blurt out the lie as though my life depends on it.

His expression turns smug when he tips his head up and glances at the corner of the room. "The video footage says otherwise."

My eyes widen and I take in a quick breath. "You have a human cage in your room and video?" I ask, tears teasing the corners of my eyes as the image I've created of this perfect man shatters.

"I do. Would you like me to show you what I saw?"

"No, I'd rather go home."

His body stiffens at my words, and he's silent for a beat but then recovers, gripping me by the arm and leading me out. "I'll take you."

"Thank you, but I'd rather call a pickup service."

"I'm not letting you head home alone. If not me, then Jake, my limo driver, will take you, but I need to make a few things clear with you before I call him."

I eye him cautiously, wondering what he

could possibly have to say that would make leaving any easier. It's stupid but I agree. "Okay."

"I've had a taste of you, and it's enough to convince me I want more. In fact, the thought of tasting you in other ways has me so fucking hard right now. But if you think what you saw is a bad thing, then you're not ready, because once I start, I'm not sure I'll be able to stop. I realize all of this is intimidating for someone in your position, may even scare you, but that's not how it's intended. Winsley, I can take your body places you've never dreamed of." He cups my chin again and heat covers my whole body. "I can make you fly."

His words send a flutter straight to my core. Giving myself to him would be more than an honor, I'm just not sure I'm experienced enough for what he wants. Especially after what I saw.

"If you need some time, I can give you that, but not much and it would be with one condition."

"What's that?" I ask breathily.

"You save your virginity for me."

CHAPTER THIRTEEN
Tinka

I WATCH HER STEP FROM THE BUILDING WITH Jake, and it takes all my willpower to stay hidden in the car. I've been sitting out here for at least an hour waiting.

When we'd driven by earlier and Preston was rushing through the double doors, I knew something was up. She was there, which meant I would be too. Whatever had gone on behind that closed door before I'd arrived wasn't just an innocent meeting after a wild afternoon at the café. No, the evidence was clear on her fucking swollen lips.

"Follow her!" I growl out, my tone that of a woman possessed and surprises even me.

The driver does as he's told, turning the Jag

around in the middle of the street and it doesn't take much to catch up to the long black car. We weave in and out of traffic and turn a couple of blocks before I realize where she's headed. Back to the café.

Once she's in what must be her own vehicle, we're back on the road again, following a few car lengths back.

It's not long before the elegant glass office buildings and high-end clothing stores disappear, and ratty ancient brick ones take over the streets. They're covered in ivy and a few have broken windows, but that's not the worst part. Trash blows around on the sidewalk and sits in the gutters.

This neighborhood sends a shiver up my spine and I can't believe anyone, especially someone Preston has his eye on, would live here. Maybe I'm jumping to conclusions. Maybe she's taking a short cut to some million-dollar neighborhood up north.

No sooner than the words leave my lips, she pulls into a deserted parking lot, exits her car, and walks across the street. Her destination, one of those eerie brick buildings.

With only four stories, it extends half a block and is surrounded by alleys and several other buildings of a similar size. But the most interesting thing about each of them is they all have old metal fire escapes outside the windows. If they weren't so disgustingly dirty, they'd be beautiful pieces of art from an era gone by.

Distracted by my sightseeing, I don't see her disappear inside. Since I'm here, I may as well go inside and warn her to stay away from him.

Tapping out Shawn's number and placing the phone to my ear, I wait for him to answer. It doesn't take but two rings before his tone slithers into my ear for the second time today. "Hey, Baby…."

"Did you find out anything?" I ask, scanning each of the windows from the first story to the fourth.

"How about you come over and I'll give you everything I know?"

"Shawn, I'm not playing games here. In fact, I'm outside of her building now, I just need to know which apartment it is."

He takes in a sharp breath. "Tinka, are you sure you know what you're doing?"

"Just give me the goddamn number," I spit, adrenaline building in my veins, pumping at a speed that sets my skin on fire.

"302 A. Let me know if you need any…"

With no more use for him, I disconnect the call and glance over at the windows once again. The way they're positioned look like eyes into a dark soul. One I'm still not convinced I want to enter, but I know she's in there somewhere. "If she can do it, then so can I." Dropping the divider I meet the driver's eyes once again. "There's someone in there I need to talk with."

He glances at the building and then back at me. "I'll come with you."

"No. It's okay, Rook is already there, I'll be fine," I inadvertently admit, but quickly realize what I've done. Pulling a small compact from my purse, I pretend to check my hair and makeup as though I didn't just out my accomplice.

When I take the mirror away, his narrowed stare is on me and I expel a breath. "I'll be fine, you can go," I tell him.

He exits the car and comes around to my side, opening my door and extending a hand to help me out. His grip is strong, and his hands are smooth, I almost reconsider bringing him along, but this is something I should do alone.

There's no way she'll even consider giving me a ride, but I'm not concerned, I have a list of trustworthy souls who'd be more than willing to pick me up.

I can feel his eyes on me as I make my way across the street. The adrenaline from earlier pumping ten times what it was before. It feels as though my veins are about to explode by the time I reach the exterior door.

The driver still waits for me on the street and I wave him away. Once he's gone, I notice the security keypad on the door. I raise my finger to press the call button for her place when someone comes bounding down the stairs with a dog.

When they push their way out, I step inside before the door closes.

It's darker than I expected but isn't as bad as I thought on the inside. The walls are a pale green and extend down a long passageway, illuminated only by brass sconces as they make their way upward at an angle with the stairs.

Placing a hand on the rail I glance up before

placing a foot on the first step.

CHAPTER FOURTEEN
Winsley

I<small>T'S NOT UNTIL</small> I'<small>M BACK AT MY APARTMENT</small> and have closed and locked the door that I breathe a sigh of relief. "What have I gotten myself into?" I ask aloud, breaking the silence of my otherwise quiet apartment. After all this time, I should know better than going along with any of Jennifer's schemes.

She'll never believe any of this.

I laugh at the ridiculousness of it all, I'll admit I was scared back at the café. When Rook grabbed my wrist and wouldn't let go, a twinge of panic had settled in. I rub my wrist where the bruise is.

I'm thankful for Preston stepping in but knowing what I know now, could the hero be just as bad?

Parts of me want to find out everything, while my brain—which is what I should be listening to—is telling me to stay away.

On second thought, she probably will.

Swiping my phone from the counter, I swipe the contact list until I find her name and tap her shining face on the screen. It rings once before her cheery voice floats through from the other side. "Win! How'd it go today?"

Just hearing her voice sets my mind at ease. I'm so ready to dump all of the day's activities on her, but on the flip side some of it I want only for myself. "Jen, if I tell you, you're not going to believe any of it."

"That bad? Just tell me who I should cut, and I'll do it."

"And that's why I love you." I letting out a breath, my tone turns serious. "I take it you haven't seen the video?"

"Video? What video?" Her voice raises an octave. "They didn't make you disrobe or anything, did they?"

"What? No? Ew… Why would you ask that?" I counter, shaking my head and rolling my eyes. "Hold on, I'll send it to you." My fingers tap away at the screen and in seconds there's a ding on the other end.

"Watch it, then call me right back."

She doesn't say anything before disconnecting the line; I turn my phone and stare at the blank screen. "Well, goodbye to you too."

It's not but three minutes before she calls back. "What the fuck happened today? Are you okay?" she screeches into the phone. "I'm coming over."

"I'm fine. It was an interesting day for sure, but you don't need to." I tell her, while the growl in my stomach is a reminder the lunch we were supposed to be eating is probably sitting in a random trashcan right now. "I think I'll just head out, grab some dinner, and then pass out in my bed."

"You know I'll not take no for an answer," she says matter-of-factly.

My side of the line goes quiet because I'm trying to think of a nice way to tell her I'm not up for company, but I've got to tell someone this news. Deciding to spend some time with my best friend may be just what I need, so I ask, "Pizza night in?"

"Done, I'll be over in forty-five," she says, clapping at the other end of the line before she excitedly responds. "I'll bring the ice cream."

"Don't take too long, I'm starving."

"Jen…Out," she says and disconnects the line.

Not having one thread of her energy, I drop my head back to the couch and close my eyes, but it's only for a moment before the chime on my cell startles me. It's probably Jen telling me she's changed her mind, but when I raise the screen it's from a number I don't recognize. "Hello?" I answer.

"Winsley." His voice floats through the line like smooth caramel, instantly raising chill bumps on my skin. There's no doubt who it belongs to.

"Preston." I relax my tone so as not to give away my excitement. "I would ask how you got my number, but I suspect a man of your talents has his ways."

"Ah yes, obtaining numbers and stalking women such as yourself are just two of my many talents," he says, his tone lighthearted and fun even.

"Is that humor I detect in your tone? Did Preston Pace just make a joke?" I ask, adding a bit of my own.

"I have my moments. But in all seriousness, I'd like to get back to the question at hand. I haven't been able to concentrate on anything else all day. Your taste has lingered on my lips and your scent on my clothes. It's a fucking distraction." He lets out a deep breath before continuing. "Have you given any thought to our earlier conversation?"

His question is all I've thought about, but I don't want to seem too eager. Even though that's exactly what I am. "I have, I just haven't made a decision yet."

"One thing I will not tolerate, Winsley, is deceit. I believe you have decided. Even if you're not ready to admit it, I know," he says, his tone hard.

He has no idea. I want to admit it, but not now. Not until my full attention can be on him and talking through what this means for the both of us. "I need more time, Preston. It's not something I'll willingly jump right into, especially with someone who…likes the things you do," I tell him, lowering my eyes to the red cocktail dress I've had on since this morning, picking at the material.

"Winsley, those things are for you as much as they are for me. I would be honored for you to give yourself to me, and I don't only mean your innocence. I mean your whole self. You would have the power, just like now. But don't take that as I'm a patient man, because I'm not. I'll only wait so long before the decision is no longer yours."

I'm not sure what that really means. Would he take me by force? I'm about to ask when there's a knock at the door. It's both a relief and a concern. Jennifer can't be here already.

"Are you still there?" His voice now low and gravelly.

"Yeah, someone's at the door. One sec." Taking the phone away from my ear, I head in that direction and glance through the peephole. "What is she doing here?" I mutter.

Flipping the three deadbolt locks, I work my way down to the knob and pull the door open.

When there's only enough space for a hand do fit through, she shoves the heavy steel against me and steps into my home, uninvited.

"What are you doing here, Tinka?" I ask, still holding the door open, hoping she'll get the hint and leave.

"Well…" she says, glancing around the room with a scrunched nose before her eyes meet mine. "I've come here to warn you to stay away from Preston."

She has nerve, I'll give her that. "I'm not too fond of anyone forcing their way into my home and warning me to do anything. Plus, if I remember correctly, the last time we talked you admitted the two of you were no longer together, which means he's fair game. So tell me, Tinka, what makes you think you have control over anything he and I do?"

"I'm glad you asked." She glances behind me.

I turn, following her gaze. My eyes go wide when I see Rook standing behind me.

He's gripping a piece of lumber and before I have a chance to react, the wood connects with the side of my head and blackness instantly spills into my vision. I drop to the floor.

CHAPTER FIFTEEN
Rook

SLINK IN FROM THE BEDROOM WITH A SMALL wooden beam. One she'd used to prop her window open. Her mindlessness has given me the opportunity to sneak in and wait for her return. She should've known better, especially in this neighborhood.

Ascending the fire escape had been risky. It wasn't just because I was out in the open for anyone from the ground and any of her neighbors to see, but it was also unstable. There's no telling the last time it'd been serviced.

Thankful for the stable ground when I'd climbed through the window, I'd expelled a breath that could've blown out a thousand candles and had even been tempted to kiss the floor, but after looking at it, falling three flights of metal stairs seemed safer than catching who knows what from the carpet in this dump.

I squat down next to her, brushing a piece of blonde hair from her face and listening for her breaths.

"Oh the fun we're going to have with you," I whisper to her lifeless body. Once the infamous Preston Pace finds out what we've done, he'll want nothing more to do with her. That's just the type of man he is. For me, it will be the sweetest revenge.

"How long will she be out?" Tinka asks, sauntering farther in the room.

"I have no fucking idea, which is why we need to get her somewhere before she wakes up and before anyone notices." Flipping her onto her stomach I pause a moment, relishing how the red dress has ridden up over her ass. The thong she wears exposes bare cheeks of a perfectly round ass and I reach out my hand, hovering for only a moment before I'm eventually hit in the face with cloth and a rope.

"You can fuck her later. As you said, we need to do something with her before anyone realizes."

I focus a narrow stare on her before turning my attention back to the beauty lying motionless on the floor.

There's really no comparison between the two.

Tinka is beautiful, but her values are all fucked up. In everyone's eyes, she expects to be treated like a princess, and most do. But Winsley, even after only knowing her a short period of time, it's clear there's beauty both inside and out.

And now, she's mine.

Gathering her hand hands behind her, I weave rope in and out between her wrists then do the same with her ankles. Just as I'm about to tighten the last knot, I notice the phone by her head. It never disconnected. Cautiously I lift it to my ear. It's a stupid move but feels robotic, almost like I want to talk to him. Like I want him to know it's me taking the girl he obviously wants. "Hello, Preston."

"Rook? You motherfu…"

Launching the phone across the room, it crashes against the wall and shatters into broken plastic and glass. It's the best feeling in the world, not listening to any more of his constant demands. Something I hadn't missed while I was away.

Although he thinks so, I wasn't the only reason *Brothers Reunited* tanked. He knew I hadn't been acting long, yet he still insisted everything we did had to be perfect. If that meant working past midnight for a scene then that's what we did. But once he'd been coined "The King of the Big Screen" nothing I did was ever good enough for him.

I needed a mentor, not a micro manager, and definitely not an asshole for a costar. It left me in a dark light; one I didn't need right out of the gate in this business. Now it's my turn. I'm taking the limelight. If that's by the media as a kidnapper, then so be it.

Ensuring her eyes are hidden beneath the cloth, I tie the ends off and take a step back.

It's ironic really, looking at her now. She's helpless. All this time I've been judging Preston's need for tying women up, yet all I can think about in this moment is I could do whatever the fuck I wanted to her right now.

"Rook, we really should go," Tinka says, breaking up my thoughts.

"Go? We're not going anywhere," I tell her. "He'll show up eventually and when he does…" I glance back down, imagining all the things I have planned for her. Her ass is where I should start but then decide that's something I'd like to save for last. And the only way I'll get anything from that mouth is if I have some help.

I lift my eyes to Tinka.

"And when he does, then what? He'll not have anything to do with us." Her brows furrow and her arms cross. "Why are you looking at me like that"

"Close the door," I demand, taking my gaze from her head to her six-inch heels.

She's yet to recognize my intentions. "Why should we wait for him, let's just get the fuck out of here." She bitches the entire way to the door and back. "And I'm not sure where you get off giving the orders."

"Can you carry her?" I ask, glancing at her from my position on the floor.

Tinka looks from Winsley to me. "Fine, just next time try being a little nicer."

"Fuck, Tink. This isn't about pleasantries. We're kidnapping a person."

Perfect, it's now or never. Flipping her back over, I place my hands behind her shoulders and legs and prepare to lift, but when I do her body stirs and she groans. Not fully awake now but once she is, her awkward position will make carrying her to the bedroom a challenge.

No sooner than the thought enters my mind, she realizes her hands are bound, and she struggles—hard.

"A little help here," I tell Tinka, barely balancing Winsley on my arms.

"What do you expect me to do?" She narrows her stare on the squirming pile of flesh.

"Grab her feet, we're taking her to the bedroom."

Tinka creases her face as she grabs the rope-covered ankles, and I reposition myself around to Winsley's shoulders. She's almost fully awake now and bucking like a wild bronco. It was a good idea for Tinka to suggest the gag because she's a screamer.

We toss her on the bed like you would a child and I begin looking for ways to strap her down. "Go lock the door, I think I'd heard her chatting with her friend on the phone. With it broken, we've no way to convince her this one…" I glance at Winsley moving about on the bed, "is off doing other things."

She leaves the room and it's my chance to get a closer look at the feast beneath the little red dress. I grab the hem and begin sliding it up her body. She's rolling to her side and away from me. But what she doesn't realize is this view is just as good as when she's lying on her back.

She bucks some more and I rise to my feet whispering, "If you don't stop moving, the Buck knife sitting on the nightstand is going straight in your kidney."

It works; she stops in an instant. There is no Buck knife but she doesn't know that. If there were it would make getting her out of that dress all that much easier. Instead I grip the material and rip it from the top to its hem. Now the only thing she should worry about is the sword in my pants. The one getting larger with each glance of her exposed skin.

Reaching out, I skim my fingertips over the smooth skin of her back and my dick hardens more, if that's even possible.

Taking her like this wasn't the plan. The plan was only a scare tactic, one Tinka had concocted as a sick way of keeping Winsley from that piece of shit Preston. But now in her compromised position, I have other ideas.

Unfastening the button of my pants, I prepare to do what I've wanted to ever since I first met the sassy young woman at a casting call.

Preston doesn't know her, not like I'm about to, but it's obvious he is into her. Which means he'll do whatever it takes to be the hero.

What he doesn't know is, I'll be waiting for him and by then it'll be too late for her.

CHAPTER SIXTEEN
Preston

THE OFFICERS LEFT AN HOUR AGO. THEY'D LET me off with a warning, agreeing that once Rook had his hand on Winsley, I'd done the right thing, albeit with excessive force.

Now in the seat next to me, Garret is frantically trying to reach those same officers again.

I'm driving at top speed to her apartment. Her address had been on the forms when she applied for the extra's role, making it easy for us to get.

"Heard anything yet?" I ask Garret, while keeping my eyes on the road and weaving through traffic.

"I wasn't able to reach Sergeant Galloway

but…" He pauses.

"But what?"

"One sec, I'm texting JR."

Out of the corner of my eye, I can see his fingers working frantically over the keys of his phone. JR is our head of security. While we have no intentions of bypassing law enforcement, he has contacts we may not be able, or can, reach out to.

"Okay, while I wasn't able to reach out to the same guys you've already talked with, JR was able to get me in touch with a detective. They're doing some investigating and will meet us at the scene when they can."

"You know she's not going to be there, right?"

"I know that. But they need to do their jobs."

I pound a hand on the steering wheel. "Why didn't she listen? Why didn't she stay away from him like I'd told her?"

"Even if she would've stayed away, I suspect it would've been the same result." He clears his throat as if he's going to say something, but doesn't.

"If you have something to say then say it."

"It's just it seems, for someone who's admitted to taking women places they've never been before, you've not realized such a simple human reaction yet."

His vague responses and assumptions about me are annoying as fuck. My response comes through gritted teeth. "Enlighten me."

"It's common knowledge, maybe even an unspoken rule, sometimes when you tell someone to do something, it makes them want to do the opposite."

The urge to pull the vehicle over and shove Garret out onto the street is overwhelming, but it would be precious time wasted, so I keep driving and defend myself verbally instead of with the fists I'd like to use.

"I believe you underestimate me on multiple levels," I say, glancing at him briefly and then back to the road. "Yes, I understand people's tendencies but there's always a reason why they choose to disobey. Finding out her reason is what I had planned to do. If she were mine, she would've listened when I told her to do something. But she wasn't. If we get her back in one piece, I'll make sure that's exactly what she'll be, even if it's the last thing I ever do."

"You're missing the point, my man."

This debate could go on and on, but it'll have to wait because we're here. Stopping in the middle of the street, I drop the luxury sedan in park and jump out. "What apartment number?"

"302 A."

I jump out of the car and rush to the door of the building. There's a keypad. "Do you know the code?" I shout at my sidekick.

He shrugs, shaking his head.

"Well, find someone who knows. Push every goddamn button on those intercoms until someone answers and lets you in. I'm going in that way." I point to the fire escape.

"How do you know which one it is?" he says, looking at the rows of four-story windows.

"I guess I'll just have to check each one until I find her."

CHAPTER SEVENTEEN
Preston

I**T'S A STUPID IDEA. H**E **KNOWS IT AND** I **KNOW IT.** I'm not even sure if the rickety steel will hold my weight but I must try. There's no telling what he's doing to her. Revenge is a strong emotion. One that can make a man do things he'd never do.

Unlatching the ladder, it comes free and slides a foot shy of the ground. I'm no religious man, but when I place my right foot on the first rung it seems like the perfect moment to utter a lifetime of prayers. "We've had our differences, but as you know, I'm trying to do a good thing here. If you can ensure I survive this death trap of metal, I'd surely appreciate it." It's nothing traditional but it'll have to do.

So far so good, I think to myself as I make it to the first platform. The rest of the way is flimsy stairs and they shake, creak, and rattle as I skip over ever other tread and make it to the next landing.

This is the third floor, but each escape only spans one apartment, which means I have six on this side and I suspect six on the other. I have a good feeling this is the right side. Peering in the first apartment window, I see children playing with blocks on a living room floor. She's a virgin, which means this is clearly not hers. The parents sitting lovingly next to one another also confirm that thought.

There's no way I'll be able to go all the way down and back up again to check each one. I'll have to climb across. Luckily the distance between each is not far, and I'm able to lean over grab the rungs from above and swing to the opposite side.

I don't land gracefully by any means, and I hold my breath as the whole escape shakes from top to bottom. My heartbeat is erratic and coursing adrenaline through my veins. This is no different than the stunts I've done in movies, and at this moment I'm thankful for the training I've had.

There's no time to stop and praise myself though. I peer in the next window. This time it's more difficult to tell. It's dark inside but not too dark to see. It could be Rook took her, which means the apartment would be empty.

In the case of this one the platform I'm on extends across to another room. A bedroom. There's a low light on and two people in bed. Clearly they're not asleep. My blood boils when the thought it could be Rook and Winsley enters my mind. These two appear to be in a very intimate relationship. She's on top and grinding against him.

My little virgin girl wouldn't be that adventurous. Not at first anyway.

I linger longer than I should. My dick is doing the thinking at this very moment. "Fuck, Preston, focus!" What was supposed to be an internal conversation is said on a shout and draws the attention of the sexy couple. Just when I think they're going to call the cops, they both turn and smile, eventually going on about their business.

Whatever apartment that is, I need to remember, because they seem like a couple I could bring home once Winsley has more experience. Not too much though. Innocence and fear can make for hot sex.

Once I'm back to the original escape and onto the next my adrenaline builds, this is the one it has to be. My instincts are confirmed when there through the window, pacing back and forth in the living area is Tinka.

I burst through the window. Glass and all.

It's not something she's ready for and she freezes mid-step. Not wasting any time, I catch her off guard, gripping her arms. "Where is she?"

"Preston, please. You don't need her. I'll do whatever you want, even that…stuff. We can leave here now and I can show you," she says, placing her hands on my waist and pleading with her eyes.

"Tink, you dug your grave in our relationship. Whatever was between us is over. Now tell me where Winsley is." I squeeze harder.

Tears tease the corners of her eyes and she lets out a shaky breath. "She's in there, probably getting fucked by Rook."

Those words set me on fire and I shove her aside, headed for the bedroom door. It's the last inanimate object separating us. Grabbing my hands together, I don't bother with the knob; instead I go at the door full force with my shoulder. It pops off the hinges with ease.

Rushing in, I could've never prepared myself for what I'm seeing.

She's on her stomach and bound at the wrist and ankles, both of which are fastened to the bed with longer rope. Her dress lies in puddles on either side, and her face is blindfolded while she's screaming into a gag as Rook is pounding her from behind.

The sight sends enough rage flowing through me that I could light the entire city of LA with a touch of my finger. I run full force at him, knocking him off her, and we tumble out of the bedroom window landing in a pile on the fire escape.

It creaks from our weight and fists flying.

I shouldn't be out here. I should be tending to Winsley and not leaving her to... "Tinka, fuck." They're the last words I say before deciding to end this for good.

Rook makes another move, trying to sweep my feet from under me but I stand, and instead stomp on his semi-hard dick.

He screams, holding himself and rolling from side to side.

The escape creaks louder and begins pulling away from the building, noticeable by the dust falling from above.

It's going down and if I don't do something quick, I'll surely be going down with it. Rook can rot in hell for all I care. I leap for the window, capturing enough of the edge to get a good grip. The sudden movement pulls the bolts from the brick building and the escape falls the three stories, landing with a loud crash and a cloud of dust. Pieces of broken glass cut into my fingers but it's better than the alternative.

Rooks broken body lies motionless atop all the metal below.

Once I find the windowsill, I grip onto the trim, and pull myself up, climbing back into the room. I'll never complain about daily chin-ups again. With no time for catching my breath, I drop to my knees beside the bed and fumble with the ends of the rope until she's free.

Next comes the blindfold, soaked with her tears, and the gag leaving streams of saliva when I remove it from her mouth. Blinking rapidly her eyes slowly adjust to the dim light. Once she recognizes who I am, she wraps her arms around my neck, and I pull her body against me. Her earlier tears now a flood wetting my shoulder.

If I thought seeing her in such a physically emotional state was hard, hearing her weak voice mutter over and over about how much it hurts rips my heart straight in half.

How will she ever recover from her innocence taken from her so forcefully and by a man with such evil inside? The only thing I can do is offer words of comfort while smoothing her hair. "I promise, when you're ready, the next time will be the highest pleasure you'd never think you could ever experience. Winsley, I want to make you fly."

Still in tremendous pain, she repositions herself; managing to take a breath and slow her tears long enough to tell me, "He did it in my ass, Preston." More tears fall. "It was like I was being ripped in two."

Where he did it shouldn't matter, and it doesn't to me, other than what he put her through. I would've made soft love to her whether it was her first time or only her first time with me.

There are very few words that will comfort her now, but there are things that need to be said. "I'm so sorry he did this to you. I should've seen it coming. I should've been here for you."

She cups the side of my face, sniffling. "It's not your fault."

"Some of it is, but, sweetheart, I'm here for you now and hopefully in the future, if you'll have me. But first we need to get you to the hospital."

No sooner than the words leave my mouth, the police stalk into the room with guns drawn. When they've determined it's only the two of us in the bedroom, they holster their weapons and come check on Winsley.

"The cavalry is here," I tell her then glance up at the officers. "She'll need an ambulance."

One of them nods and is quick to radio it in via his walkie, while the other kneels down beside us and we fill him in on what happened.

The scene that played out here is like a real-life version of a movie but not a role I'd planned on taking with her. I'm ready for where things take us next.

Once everything has been explained to the police, with Winsley in my arms, we take an elevator ride down three stories and then exit the building. Looking at the scene there are fire trucks, an ambulance, and more than four police cars, one of which Tinka currently sits in the back of.

She was there and she didn't try to stop him, it makes me think she played a big role in what went down. I'll get the detail from Garret later, right now Winsley needs medical attention. Just as I'm preparing to hand her off to the EMTs, a young woman rushes over to us.

Her face is flushed with panic and her bags of what look to be groceries crash to the ground. "Winsley? Oh my God, what happened to you?" she asks, about to place her hands on my woman when I turn away from her.

"And you are?" I ask sternly.

"I'm Jennifer, her best friend," she spits

back.

I glance from the stranger and back to Winsley. She nods and more tears escape.

Turning back to who I now know as Jennifer, I tell her, "It's a long story, one we don't have time for right now. The ambulance is taking her to the hospital. If you want, you can ride with my agent, Garret." I nod behind her. "He's headed there now and we can fill you in once this one is stable.

"You got it, boss. This way, Miss Jennifer."

"Thank you," she says, before turning back to us and placing a hand on Winsley's arm. "We'll be right there, hon.."

Winsley offers her friend a tired nod then adjusts herself in my arms and leans her head against my chest.

Once she's in the ambulance, settled in the gurney, and I'm by her side; she turns to me and the last words out of her mouth before they cover her face with an oxygen mask make my heart swell.

"Preston, I was going to tell you tomorrow but then all this happened." She takes my hand in hers. "I've made my decision, and my answer is I want you. All of you."

Epilogue

Six months later…

THE DOCTOR SAID SIX MONTHS WOULD BE enough time for my infection to clear up and the tears on my ass to heal.

It was tough going there for a time because not only did the infection get so bad it settled in my body, but it had taken almost a month of being hooked up on an IV filled with antibiotics that ultimately saved my life.

Preston couldn't say enough kind things about the doctors and nurses who treated me. They were on par and the kindest people the entire time he'd said. I was being treated like his queen.

"You know that today is?" I ask, giving him my best sultry eyes and a little more cleavage than normal.

"Yes," he says nonchalantly, his indifference at my blatant hints driving me crazy.

"I'm ready, Preston," I plead.

"I don't know, Winsley. Isn't it a day before your six months is up?" He's teasing me and I'm not finding it humorous. I am ready for him to fuck me hard and fast and then do it again, slowly and torturously.

We've played around before but have always been gentle and cautious of my injuries. Never quite bringing me to orgasm, which means I'll probably explode as soon as he touches me down there.

"Preston…" I say, pushing his newspaper down, trying to get his attention.

"Yes," he says, ignoring my pleas and lifting his paper back up

"Come on, you promised." I give him my best puppy eyes, knowing they're the ones he can't resist.

Without warning, he turns over in the bed and quickly takes my chin between his thumb and forefinger before giving me a warning. "Don't play games with me, Winsley."

I brush his hand away and laugh. "You know that doesn't work on me anymore, right?"

He does know. But he also knows how to win a battle. He drops his lips to mine. Teasing me at first, then taking me to a peak where the only release would be an orgasm. Something I'm ready for now more than I have ever been.

His gaze is eating up every inch of my body like I'm the last meal on earth. The only one for him.

Tucking a wisp of hair behind my ear, he leans in, pressing his lips to mine. If heaven were a place on earth, it would be the softness of those very lips.

Returning the intensity he gives so easily, and a deep growl permeates from his chest. Here we meld seamlessly. Our lips, the emotion and need pouring from the other. It's an ache I've never experienced before.

"Winsley...Stay with me," he says, his soft tone filled with control.

We're both naked, he'd made that a rule as soon as I'd come to live with him. Neither of us wear clothes in the bedroom. There's no point, they're just getting pulled off anyway.

"There is one thing I'm changing about tonight. You start playing with your clit. I need to grab something," he warns.

"Oh really?" With his *preferences* it could be anything and my nerves suddenly stand on edge, sending chill bumps over my skin. Nevertheless, I slide my fingers over myself just as he'd asked.

When he's almost to the bed, he tosses my cat with the Christmas hat T-shirt at my face. "Don't get spoiled with this. I'm only allowing you the opportunity to wear this shirt one night because I promised myself that's what I'd do."

I'm ecstatic about the shirt, but he doesn't give me much time slip it on because he's kneading my breasts and pinching at my nipples, making me groan.

"Hmm, I could taste this beautiful body forever," he says, placing his lips to my neck and running his tongue over her skin. His tongue is like licks of fire and he's burning my skin with each and every touch. It's only a short time before he's made his way to my collarbone and further south, eventually suckling on one of her nipples.

His hands grip my waist.

This is a new experience for me. And I'm loving EVERY FUCKING MINUTE of it.

My belly is now being assaulted by his tongue, toying with my belly button. It makes me giggle and I squirm.

"Shhh," he says. "No squirming. If I have to tell you not to move again, it will come with a punishment."

His commanding tone sets my blood on fire, making me wetter than I already am. In my fantasies I've always wanted a man in control. Especially one who is a good teacher and teaches me the way he likes things.

Slowly he drags his tongue from my belly to my pelvic bone, positioning himself between my legs and I stiffen my knees. What if he doesn't like what he sees? What if I'm not as pretty as Tinka...down there? He might change his mind and leave.

Oh God, he can't leave.

"Winsley," his tone demands. "Open your legs for me. I want to see how beautiful you are everywhere."

I hesitate.

"Come on, sweetheart, open yourself to me. I want to take in every inch of you. I want to taste you."

My knees spread barely.

"That's right, a little more. I'm not going to force you. I want you to do it for me, and for yourself." He's quickly melting my psyche.

I relax, allowing my thighs to drop on the soft cloud, which is his bed beneath.

"Beautiful" he says, leaning closer. His warm breath heats parts of me I've never exposed to another. It's a rush of him being so close, and the anticipation of his touch. But nothing could've prepared me for what he does next.

With one swipe of his tongue, I'm lost. It's magical a mix of heat and chills over my skin, forcing an ache to build that could explode any minute. Preston is everything I thought he would be: kind, gentle, and a lot controlling.

There's no way I can keep from arching my back. I'm so close to letting it all go, I want it to last longer, but he's taking me so high I feel like I could be flying right along with the very white puffs my mind is drifting to.

When I said slow and torturous, I never thought it would be like this. "Preston, please I want you to make me come."

He's still for the longest time, as though he's considering my plea but doesn't say as much. After a beat he lowers his tone. "Are you sure you're ready?"

"Yes. Please. What if tomorrow I die and I never get the opportunity of having Preston Pace inside of me?" I say on a long breath. I face away from him, unsure what might be going through his mind, and not wanting to know if I'll be rejected. But the next words out of his mouth are like a godsend.

"Lie back."

I do as he asks.

"Close your eyes."

The softness in his tone is slowly lulling me into a headspace where it's only him.

"I'm going to slip my finger inside. Focus your mind on how my touch feels," he rumbles.

His finger doesn't go far and even though I try, I'm having a hard time getting past thoughts of the barrier keeping him from me. It's not until the he begins a rhythmic pace that I'm able to push out all the thoughts in my head except for what he's doing.

Now is when I realize I want *him*—all of him. I moan.

"Shhh, quiet. Think about the sensation, the need building in your pussy and expanding to every nerve. Can you feel it, Winsley, the mountain I'm building?"

"Yes, I feel it."

Repositioning himself between my legs, he takes my hand and places my own fingers on my pussy while he aligns his dick with my entrance and leans in close. "You know what's on the other side of a mountain, Winsley?"

"Yes." I respond breathily, my fingers working faster.

"You're at the top, sweetheart. Take us over that cliff." With that I shout out and he forces himself inside.

My innocence is lost but my love for this man will never be.

THE END

THE CURSE BEHIND THE MASK

sneak peek

I'm no Prince Charming. I'm your worst nightmare.

Tonight, at the erotic masquerade ball, I get to choose a girl to play with. She'll endure my deepest, darkest, erotic pleasures.

I'll ruin her for any other man, push her limits.

I finally see her, a beautiful brunette, her body made for me. She must play my game, submit to my demands under the watchful eye of the evil queen, if she wants to survive.

CHAPTER ONE
Elijah

I STOOD WITH MY HANDS ON THE BALCONY overlooking the foyer, I stare down and stalk the women as they entered the house to attend tonight's Erotic Masquerade Ball. The men were dressed in tuxedos and the ladies in glamorous dresses, all aware of the sick adventures they were about to enjoy. You had to be crazy to attend these parties, and I, for one loved to torment and defile a woman as much as anyone else. I'm a prince, after all, bad behaviour was a given. I was not made to adhere to the stuck up, clean cut arsehole persona that was expected. That was not me.

I consider myself a monster, a devil, a ruthless, powerful man who can do what I want, when and how I wish. I don't care what happens at these parties, as long as they all get what they want, sexual gratification. I have the women bowing at my feet, even the unwilling become willing.

Sex, I love it — the more deviant, bloodthirsty, and shameful the better.

I wore an elegant black suit with a high collar to show my authority, a dark silk tie that would come in use later, and a custom-made gold warrior mask.

I watch as the guests were scanned for weapons then taken to the booths for headshots, for identification reasons, if required. Those were the rules, my rules, no room for negotiations.

I liked to watch the girls enter to see who took my attention and made my dick hard. I had to choose wisely. I have a reputation to uphold, and the woman I select must be able to keep up and be ready for pain and degradation, without a damn clue about who I was.

I used to do these parties without masks, and all the girls flocked to my feet and begged me to use and abuse them like I was God. I learned my lesson, and now…masks were to be worn until the guests were shown to their rooms for their pleasure.

Once security cleared them, they were each offered a glass of cava before they proceeded to the grand hall and to take part in any events they wish.

I observed the ladies and did a double-take when the most stunning woman walked through the large door. My breath hitched. She wore a fitted gold dress that sparkled, dazzling my eyes. Her body was stupendous, slender and divine, her long dark hair fell in loose waves. A mask covered half her face, leaving her mouth exposed and right then…I wanted to kiss her red lips.

She entered the booth, and I eagerly watched for her to emerge.

Soon the beauty exited the booth, and like a breath of fresh air, she moved to take a glass of the cava. She looked around the grand foyer to take in her surroundings. I watched as she trailed down the rounded staircase, and lifted her head, before tilting it back to look at the painted ceiling of hell, showing death, the grim reaper, and all the pain and despair that fiery pit held.

Her eyes magically found mine. She stilled, to gaze at me for a few seconds. My dick pressed firmly against my slack zipper, begging to come out and play.

Much to my annoyance, security moved her along. She glanced back at me briefly before she walked forward and disappeared from my sights.

I rushed down the staircase, I had to get to her before anyone else did. I bowed my head to greet the guests as I passed. I wasn't going to speak; I didn't need to.

Inside the booth, I whispered to the photographer… "The girl in a sparkling gold dress who was just in here."

"Yes, Sir."

"Information," I ordered.

He moved to the computer and scrolled up the list, and there she was, her face was beautiful. Her brown eyes hypnotised me and sent pulses to my dick.

"Tell me she's single?"

"She's single."

I grinned, delighted with the result. I smirked

with thoughts of her and what pleasure I was going to have with her body. I stepped away from the booth and pressed my hands together, thinking of my desired plans for her. The first thing was to get closer, examine, devour and bring her to her knees. She was mine, and no one else was to touch her. I plan to make her scream her orgasm to the point she explodes.

I made my way to the grand hall, a spacious room with marble pillars on either side of the entrance. Tables and chairs were placed strategically, with the orchestra at one end, the walls and ceiling were painted with figures of Roman mythology, death, and betrayal. There were large chandeliers that hung above, shining on the marble floor. My chair was placed at the opposite side of the hall but I had no plans to sit there, none at all. I wanted to keep my guests guessing where the devil prince was.

I made my way around the hall in slow motion as the orchestra played, bellowing out their classic orchestrated music blissfully. Each piece was carefully selected for the evening.

I moved between guests, in an attempt to find her. All the women wore masks and glorious sexy dresses, some covered more flesh than others. I was on a hunt, where was this single woman who would be my feast for the evening, and she had no idea. The music forced me to feel its power racing through my soul as my heart pounded against my chest wall. I was eager to find her and claim her before another.

Shadily, I move through the guests, I smiled and nodded to be polite; but my eyes only searched for her. She appeared to have disappeared into thin air.

I moved to the centre of the room, my eyes sweeping the area so fast it seemed the room was spinning.

A new piece started to play, and within seconds the ballroom floor was littered with guests, they embrace and move to the flow of the orchestra.

I moved aside and once again went in pursuit of her. How the hell could she be that difficult to find?

I did my best to avoid getting in the way of the dancers. I heaved in a deep breath, and then I spotted a sparkling gold dress behind a pillar. I moved toward her in a heartbeat; only much to my surprise, it was a different woman. I smiled at the woman before moving on.

This was like a game of hide-and-seek, only I was the one hunting, and she was the one giggling somewhere in delight that I could not find her. This was not her game to play. I was the one who held all the damn commands not her. I clenched my fists and released them when I spotted her from the corner of my eye, standing across the ballroom. I stared at her, afraid to take my gaze off her in case I lost her again. She had no escape this time.

In an expeditious movement, I strode to her side of the hall and was about to make my swoop, when a waiter offered me a glass of cava. I took one and swiftly moved behind her. She must have sensed me. She turned slightly glancing over her shoulder.

I smiled down at her; I knew how beautiful she was under that mask. My dick throbbed; the music played in sync with the beat of my heart. I moved back slightly, and she studied me, not taking those breath-taking eyes off me.

I swallowed and saw the Queen, her blonde hair flowing, evil eyes painted in different shades of pink and blue, her mask was a skeletal jaw from her nose downwards, her silver dress covered tiny parts of her slim body. She was seated in her chair beside where I was meant to be, only she would be sitting alone. Her guards took their positions behind her, wearing leather kilts and armour down one arm, bare-chested.

My attention was thrown back to the girl, my mission, to take this brunette from every orifice. She was in for trouble, and if she wished to survive the night, she needed to get out now.

The music played; guests danced elegantly across the ballroom.

I looked at her, as she watched the dancers, floating around the floor in perfection.

They stopped when the music paused, only for the Waltz to erupt, my favourite ballroom dance. My mother taught me this dance when a child before she died in a terrible accident that caused her to drown in the lake. Each time I heard this symphony I thought of her.

There was no time to dwell on the past. A man was talking to her. I swooped in and interrupted.

"May I have this dance?" I reached out my

hand and bowed.

I lowered my head before lifting to find her eyes on me.

"I don't know how to," she spoke sweetly, her voice stole another ounce of my sanity.

"I'll guide you," I offered, not believing this woman had no idea how to Waltz, but then, not everyone had been as lucky as me to be brought up with money and power. I waved my hand to her, encouraging her to take it.

She licked her lips and scanned the dancefloor before her eyes met mine. I offered her my hand once again. She had to take it in order for me to make her mine for the night. There was no way she would go to another. I wanted her on my St Andrews Cross, there were torture apparatuses just for this occasion.

Once in the middle of the ballroom floor, I placed my free hand on her lower back.

"Keep looking into my eyes," I ordered.

I lifted her onto my feet, and she gasped and her eyes widened. I smiled and she returned it. We started moving about the floor. I didn't falter once, continuing to move as I gazed into her eyes. I pictured the pretty woman I'd seen earlier on the computer screen. In a few elegant swoops, we moved around the floor in time to the music. My heart raced in my chest. I moved her to the ground, then spun her around, and brought her back into my chest. She fell into step, and we danced like the wind about the floor. I made certain she focused, and I held her tight around her tiny waist, guiding her to make sure I didn't make a show of the fact that this was her first Waltz. I was completely transfixed by everything about her, her eyes, her scent, her hair. I would dump her in a split-second if I wasn't.

I had no time to mess about. I expected my woman to be perfect at everything, like the women I had in the past, older, younger, whatever stole my fancy. I like a woman with power who loved the sadistic man I was. I was no damn prince charming, if anything, I was a man who thrived on pain.

I had her.

She was mine.

With each motion, her body called to me. I hoped she was ready to lose that dress and have the night of her life, one that would change her forever. I had plans. She was the plan. She was going to be my fulfillment.

The Queen watched me dance with the woman, and I knew what she was thinking. She was the one who held all the cards tonight. She was the one who set the challenges, fulfilling our darkest fantasies.

The air in the room filled with dry ice, the lights were dimmed, and the night was unfolding. I grew hornier by the minute, eager to get on with tonight's thrill. I would steal every ounce of the woman's purity and ruin her opinion of sex in the future. I would mark her, bleed her dry, make her weep in ways that corrupt her mind. She would be scarred, left weak and of no use to anyone.

I was sick, deranged, a menacing man with bizarre erotic desires. I had my easy little bitches, and once I was done with them, I threw them away like scrap, to the hounds. I had no remorse and no control. The Queen made me this, a sick fucker. She taught me all the games, introduced me to the world of BDSM and sadism. I could not count the times she'd put me under her hypnotic control and forced me into this dark world, and …I was now addicted. It was her fault.

The Queen preyed on me like a hawk. I hated the woman, and she had this hold over me, a deep hold I could not get out of. She held my inheritance, this house the fortune my parents left to me. I had to be a good boy. I had to do what she told me without questions. She had me by the balls and squeezed them hard until I kneeled.

The Queen waited for me to give the nod, to tell her this girl was the one and once that happened, she would swoop the girl away to be prepared for me.

I kept my hold on the woman, gazing at her from time to time. She was so radiant, and her lips so supple and delicate. I wished to remove her mask and admire the pretty girl I saw on the photo, only not in here. I wondered how I could possibly get closer or leave the hall without the stalking eyes of the Queen. Her guards watched me; I had no goddamn chance of even taking a piss without her knowing about it.

The music ended, and she glanced around the floor to see what the other ladies were doing and like them, she positioned herself to take a curtsy as I took a bow and stood in front of her, our eyes locked. I tried not to look at the Queen aware her evil eyes were filled with darkness, and I felt it too.

My heart thumped hard against my chest, and the saying *treat her mean, make her keen* came to mind.

"Thank you for the dance." It took everything in me to walk away from the mystery woman, but I knew that if this night were to go to plan, I needed to move away from her.

I walked around the room and greeted regular guests of ours, a vile man who ended up killing some of his girls and another who attended every ball had a thrill to make her behave like a horse. Strange, but then, I was not one to judge.

I had to fight the desire to turn to her and see what she was doing. The woman had a hold on me. My dick throbbed and I didn't even have her stripped naked and shackled.

I was in for a serious treat tonight.

ONE CLICK NOW

ACKNOWLEDGMENTS

thank yous

I would like to thank my beta reader Ashley Cestra for her input and all around go to person!

ABOUT
the author

TL Mayhew is a Contemporary and Dark Romance
writer from Nebraska. Her love for reading started
back in elementary school when her favorite books,
The Black Stallion, Black Beauty and Misty of
Chincoteague all seemed to have one theme... a
horse as the leading character. It's fair to say that
since then her reading tastes have changed and
now, instead of a horse as the leading character it's
a hot alpha.

It wasn't until she married and had two kids, that
TL put any thought in to writing. And even then
it was close to a year before any words were put
on paper. Amazingly those words were the direct
result of a question "Do you want to give it a try?"
from an Author TL idolizes. If it weren't for that
question she may never have realized her love for
writing and wouldn't have her first work releasing
in January 2018.

ALSO BY
the author

Midwest Sins Duet

Taken
Found

Standalone
Belong
Wicked Lady T

FIND TL
online

Facebook Author Page:
https://www.facebook.com/tlmayhew

Facebook Profile:
https://bit.ly/2Kxf9Xd

Facebook Group Mayhew's Mayhem:
https://bit.ly/2KyT9vm
I
Instagram:
https://www.instagram.com/mayhewtl/

Twitter:
https://twitter.com/tmayhew

Website:
https://tlmayhew.com/

Printed in Great Britain
by Amazon

48913774R00123